I0451286

Damon

THE GRANT BROTHERS SERIES BOOK 6

KATHI S. BARTON

This is a work of fiction. Names, characters, places, and incidents are products of the author's imagination or are used factiously and are not to be construed as real. Any resemblance to actual events, locations, organizations, or person, living or dead, is entirely coincidental.

WCP

World Castle Publishing
Pensacola, Florida

Copyright © by Kathi S. Barton 2012
ISBN: 9781937593988
First Edition World Castle Publishing February 1, 2012
http://www.worldcastlepublishing.com

License Notes
This book is licensed for your personal enjoyment only. This book may not be re-sold or given away to other people. If you would like to share this book with another person, please purchase an additional copy for each recipient. If you're reading this book and did not purchase it, or it was not purchased for your use only, then please purchase your own copy. Thank you respecting the hard work of this author.

Cover: Karen Fuller
Editor: Brieanna Robertson

Dedication

To all the readers who loved the Grant Brothers as much as I did, I thank you so very much. All the men, Nicky, Devin, Spence, Byr, Jamie and Damon have touched my heart in ways that I never expected and it is so wonderful to know that you guys loved them too. But they aren't finished.

The next series I'm writing, the Waite Family has the brothers a little older but no less handsome, a little more settled but more determined to be there for the helpless and just as smart mouthed as ever. Join Cain in his fight to open a practice with his mentor Damon and his journey to win the woman who holds his heart.

Thanks again for all your support!

Kathi

Chapter 1

Connor Kirkpatrick walked along the sidewalk and kept his head down. He was cold and he was starving, but he couldn't lose focus on his mission. He'd been walking for hours and he couldn't let his mother down. She needed him and if he needed to walk more, he would.

Sitting down for a few minutes, he looked up at the street names. Some of the words were too big for his eight-year-old vocabulary, but he could make them out. His momma had been teaching him to read since he was little. When they'd gotten away this time, she said it was important to keep up with his education. Before that, she'd been too hurt to do much more than keep Mr. Ormond happy. And that wasn't all that easy or often either. The street name was High Street. The other one was…Board, no it was Broad Street. He didn't think he was ever going to find the one called North Fourth Street.

The phonebook had said there was a clinic at that street and that they would give out medicine if someone needed it. Connor wasn't sure what his momma needed, but he thought that anything was better than what she had right now, which was nothing.

He looked across the street and saw a man in a heavy coat go in a tall building with a lady. Connor thought it would be warm in there and looked to see if anyone would see him. He thought if he could just get warm for a little while then he'd have no problems going on to the other street.

He crossed at the light and made his way along the front of the building. There was a man there in a uniform and it almost made Connor turn and run in the other direction, but his back was turned as he was facing the couple. Connor pulled open the door just enough for his slight body to fit through and darted inside. As soon as he made it to the other side of the room, he slid under one of the benches. Just as he thought it would be, he was warm.

Connor huddled tight under the bench, trying to make himself as small as possible. He watched for anyone to notice him. No one seemed to have seen him, but he knew that he'd not be able to stay long. His momma needed him and he had to get back to her. The warmer he got, the drowsier he got until he fell asleep.

~~~

"Dr. Grant, it's David on the line. He is saying something about a runaway. He wants to know if you'll come down and have a look at him. He's afraid the boy looks like someone has hurt him."

"Where is he? I'm about to go out, Tansy. Can you ask him where the kid is and why he hasn't called Children's Services?" Damon just wanted to have this day end.

It had been a hell of a week and he had never been so happy to have Friday roll around. His brothers and he were going to go to dinner at his favorite restaurant and he was having a thick, juicy steak and lots of sour cream on his baked potato. He thought he might even drink a beer or two as well. It wasn't every day that one turned thirty-five.

"He said the boy is asleep under one of the benches in the lobby," Tansy told him sadly. "He said it's the holidays and he doesn't want to call Services if he doesn't have to. David is worried that the kid is hurt."

"I'll go down and see," Morgan said as she bundled up the twins. "I'm on my way out anyway. Your mother and I are going to go to the Polaris and make sure the decorations are up for the benefit in two weeks. If I have any trouble, I'll have David give you a call." Morgan moved to the elevator as she spoke.

"Thanks, sweetie. I'll make sure there is something extra special in your stocking this year. And if I can't get Nicky to get it for you, I'll get it." Damon loved his sisters-in-law, and Morgan would always have a special place in his heart.

He was going down the hall toward the elevator himself ten minutes later when his cell when off. The first thing he heard was a high-pitched scream then Morgan begging for someone to calm down. He skipped the opening doors and his brothers standing there waiting for him to enter and took off for the stairs. He would lose the connection if he took the elevator, and he was afraid of something happening.

"Damon, get down here quick. He's hurt bad and he won't let me touch him. Oh, God, Damon, someone hurt him bad," Morgan said as she came back on the line.

Damon went back up the one flight of stairs and grabbed his bag off the floor of his office. He was back down the stairs and was slamming out of the stairwell when he heard a kid scream. He knew that sound. It was pain, pain and terror. Coming out of the stairwell, he walked up to where his brothers were standing and moved his way to the front.

"Enough," Damon barked. The boy snapped his mouth closed, but he never stopped whimpering. "I'm a doctor and I'm going to see what all the shouting is about. You'll not move or you may hurt this nice lady here, you understand?"

Wide-eyed terror looked back at him. Damon saw the tiny nod of the little boy's head. He went down on his knees and made his way toward him. He could see the blood now. It pooled under him where he had been lying. Damon couldn't see where he'd been hurt, but could see enough to know it was extensive.

"This is my medical bag. These men are my brothers and they won't hurt you either. This is Spencer and Byron and my baby brother Jamie. This pretty lady is Morgan, the man behind her is another brother, Nicky. You have any brothers or sisters?"

This time, a negative shake of his head.

"My name is Damon Grant. I'm going to get a little closer to you and have a look at your arm. Don't move, I don't want you to hurt you anymore, all right?"

Damon reached slowly toward the boy and crawled on his knees a bit closer. This close, Damon could see that he was underweight and that he looked like he'd been out in the cold for a while; his lips and face were chapped.

10

Moving slowly, Damon gently wrapped his fingers around the boy's forearm and settled down on his own feet.

"Are you hungry? I can get one of them to go and get you something to eat and drink. It won't be much, just a candy bar with chocolate and a bottle of water, but they'll go get it for you now."

Damon heard one of them move and was glad they understood. He also knew that they'd bring the boy just what he'd asked for, too. He opened his bag and pulled out his stethoscope. He put it to his ears.

"I need to take your shirt off...I forgot your name."

"Connor. Connor Joshua Kirkpatrick. And I'm eight, not stupid. I want to go now, all right? I didn't take anything and my momma needs me. I have to get to the clinic for her."

"No, I can see that you're not, Connor. I'm sorry. Next time I'll be honest with you. Is your momma hurt too? Like I said, I'm a doctor. Maybe I can help her too. Can you tell me where she is? And maybe her name?"

This time, when one of his brothers moved, he knew it was to make a phone call. They would call their mom to come and help with this now. Damon smiled at Connor.

"Yes, sir. Charlotte Kirkpatrick, but everybody but the bastard calls her Charlie. But I can't take you to her. She said that we had to stay off the grind and lay low. I ain't going...I'm not going back to that man and neither is my momma."

Damon thought he meant off the grid, but thought it best not to correct him. He could see the hatred on Connor's face and wondered if this "bastard" was the one they were hiding from. He pressed the scope to Connor's chest and listened to his healthy-sounding heart and then checked his pulse. It was a little fast, but Damon figured it was because he was scared. He felt someone tap on his arm and turned to take the candy bar and bottled water from Jamie.

"You can have these as soon as I have a look at your back. Your heart is fine and your pulse is a little slow but not dangerously so. I can see that you're bleeding, Connor. Would you mind turning around for me?"

He wasn't sure he was going to do it, but he moved slowly, if not a little cautiously, to face the wall. There was a little blood on the coat, so Damon took it by the collar and pulled it off his shoulders. The shirt beneath was saturated. Morgan hissed at the sight but said nothing. Damon didn't want to hurt Connor, but the blood had dried in a few places and he was afraid it had stuck to whatever wounds were under it.

"Connor, are you bandaged up or does your shirt lie on your wounds? I need to take this shirt off, but I don't want to hurt you to do it. Some of the blood is sticking to you."

"Momma taped me up with some white material when we came through Iowa. She was hurting pretty bad by then, but she got worsted as we came over. I didn't want her to look at it no more. It made her cry."

Damon took out a pair of scissors. He decided that cutting the shirt away would be better. He nodded to Morgan who was crying softly next to him.

"Morgan has some little boys about your size and she'll give you one of their shirts when I'm finished. I'm going to cut this one off you. She's going to go and see

12

what we can find up in my office. There might be a shirt or two up there and if not, I got a few gowns we can put over you until we can replace your shirt."

Morgan's twin sons were only two years old, not nearly big enough to share a shirt with this child, but she needed something to do. And Damon wanted the boy to think everything was going fine and that he'd leave as soon as Damon was finished with him.

Cutting away the bandage and shirt was hard. The padding was thick and there was a great deal of it. When Damon finally got to his skin, it was everything he could do not to pull the little boy into his arms and hold him. He heard his brothers curse behind him and knew that they felt the same way.

The wounds were both fresh and older. Someone had taken a wide strap, probably a leather belt, to his back and had done it hard enough to draw blood. Some of the cuts oozed; a few of them bled profusely. There was bruising as well and a few of those had been caused by something wider and more blunt. Through all his examination, Connor never muttered a sound.

"He said he was going to hurt her more if I didn't lay still and take it like a man. Men don't get beat up with a belt. It's okay that he hit me when he wasn't hurting Momma. But he lied. He hurt her in places a girl shouldn't get hurt. If I ever see the bastard again, I'm gonna kill him dead."

While Connor was still turned with his back away, Damon took out a syringe and filled it with a sedative. He didn't want to harm Connor, but he needed him to be out when he had to stitch up the wounds. But he stopped short of putting the drug in the water bottle when Connor struck up a deal.

"I'll take you to my momma so you can help her, but you can't tell no one where we are. He'll find us soon enough, she said, but if she is not hurting so much then we can go faster. I got me a bat hid out, but I'm just a little kid and maybe if you help us both, we can stay gone. He told us if we run again, he was gonna kill us anyway."

"All right. You have a deal. But Connor, I want something in return. A deal is two way, right? I want you to tell me all you can about the bastard that did this to you and your momma. Because if I see him first, I'm going to be the one killing him."

Connor turned and looked at him. Then he looked at the men standing behind him. He knew they were being sized up and he had never been more proud in his life as he was at that moment. Morgan came back then and she went into Nicky's open arms and let him hold her.

"He's a mean bastard and he has a gun. He hit my momma with it one time. If he comes at you, he don't play fair. I don't want nobody to get hurt 'cause of us."

"You don't worry about us. And once our mom finds out what he's done, he won't stand a chance. She's about as mean as they come when it comes to someone hurting kids. Trust me."

"Damon Grant, what a thing to tell a young man. But he's right. And as soon as we can get it figured out, I'm going make him wish he'd never messed with what's mine. You must be Connor. My name is Margaret Parker. Let's go get your momma, shall we?"

Chapter 2

Charlotte Kirkpatrick drifted in and out of consciousness. Glad one moment for the blissfulness of the darkness and cursing it because she'd left her and her son without protection. Not that she could do much in her current state, but she still had a responsibility toward her son.

Charlotte, Charlie to her friends, had gotten further this time than she and Connor ever had before. All the way to Ohio before she had to have them get off the bus and rest. The sign with their picture on it hadn't helped either. Anthony Ormond had gone all out this time. Posters being printed cost money. Something he hated to do was spend money on anyone but himself.

Charlie was just drifting out again when she heard a noise. Connor was missing too. She tried to call for him, but the bruising around her neck made it difficult and then there were the broken ribs. When she sat up to try and go find him, pain ripped through her like a knife and brought her back down again.

Voices brought her around this time. Harsh and male mixed with the anxious voice of a woman. The room where she and Connor had been sleeping for two days was dark and smelled badly too. But there was a light nearby and the spicy scent of cologne. Expensive cologne. She was drifting out again when someone flashed a light in her eyes. When she tried to pull away from it, a man spoke softly to her.

"Mrs. Kirkpatrick? My name is Damon Grant. I have your son with me. Connor, come speak to your mother, please. Assure her that you're fine."

"Momma? I had to bring them. Dr. Damon is going to help you. He said he'd keep us off the grind until we were all better. He is real nice."

"No. We...we are okay. Must...we must get moving...hurt but fine now." She hated that she sounded weak and waited for the slap that usually accompanied her speaking without permission. But it didn't come.

"You're not okay. You've three broken ribs and I'm sure a multitude of other wounds that need immediate medical attention. Connor has to have an antibiotic and you need fluids. I'm taking you to my house where I'll care for you and your son. If you want to argue, then get up off this floor and show me how 'okay' you are."

Charlie looked up at the man and wanted to get up for no other reason than to prove him wrong and to maybe punch him in the nose. "Bastard," she mumbled. His bark of laughter startled her.

"My mother would have words with you about that term, Mrs. Kirkpatrick. She and my father were very much married when I was born. Right now she is upset with my brother Jamie because his lovely wife was very pregnant when they got married last month. Dane is due in a couple of months. In fact, all of my brothers had to beat the birth announcement with a wedding one within months of each other. Well, except for Byron, though I don't expect it to be much longer for them either."

"Not married. Never happening. Is Connor...he beat Connor. You have to see to him first. Please, he's my...please help my baby."

"Connor is just fine. I'm going to put a few stitches in his back when we get to my house. He's dehydrated too and he needs a good meal or two to get him back up to weight. He's a good boy. I'll see to him. I'm going to give you something for pain. Then we'll move you out of here. Are you allergic to anything?"

"No, nothing. Hurt bad, but Connor...please, don't let him see me. He is too young for this."

Charlie thought Connor knew more than she realized, but didn't want to think about that. In the three years they had been with Mr. Ormond, she had been beaten more than most people would believe. This was the eighth time they had escaped and knew that if he caught them this time, Ormond would kill Connor just to hurt her. She decided she would kill him first.

The tiny prick of the needle sliding into her arm had her wince then as the doctor's smooth voice spoke around her, she slipped away. She had no idea why she trusted his voice, but she did. Connor must have as well or he never would have brought him to her.

~~~

Connor watched the man pick up his momma. She looked so small in his big arms. He didn't even yell at her for being hurt or bloodying up the floor. He just wrapped her in a big cover and picked her up.

When they had set out for the building, Dr. Damon had listened to him. Connor wasn't used to that. When he spoke to Mr. O, and that wasn't often, the man would just backhand him when Connor would say more than three words. Dr. Damon had been surprised that Connor had walked so far in the cold too.

"It's nearly four miles from my office to here, Connor. I'm impressed, but you should never do that again. Someone could have taken you or hurt you. Your mother would have been in real trouble had that happened. Next time you need something, you tell me and I'll make sure you have it."

"Yes, sir. I'm sorry. My momma wasn't waking up much lately and she told me there was a clinic on North Fourth Street. I thought maybe if I got her something for the pain, she'd be able to get up again."

"You have no reason to be sorry, Connor. What you did for her is incredibly brave and smart. I didn't mean that you did anything wrong. You were man enough to know that her needing help was something you needed to take care of. I'm very proud of you. As I'm sure your mom will be too."

No one had ever been proud of Connor before and he wasn't sure what to say to that so he didn't say anything. He did keep the feeling it gave him deep in his heart so that when he was feeling bad or Mr. O found them again then, he could pull it out and feel it again. He didn't have many things he could pull out of that special place—his mother's hugs and kisses, and this thing from Dr. Damon.

He'd eaten the candy bar when they had left the office. The water was so good and cold that he had drunk it really fast. Too fast, he guessed, because it didn't stay down long. Mr. Jamie had told him not to worry about it when he helped him clean up.

"My wife is going to have a baby soon and she was always throwing up when we first got married. Never saw a woman who could eat so little and puke up twice that much. Scared me for a while. I thought she was having an alien or something. But Damon said it was a normal baby. Just between me and you, I'm still waiting for it to be born to be sure."

"My momma's friend throws up all the time. She said it's her diet. Don't know why someone would throw up on purpose, do you? It makes my belly hurt."

"Yeah, that is weird. There are a lot of odd people in the world, my man. A lot of them. Okay, you're cleaned up. I think that shirt looks good on you. I might have another one if you want it. My mom keeps everything."

Jamie's wife, Dane, brought some shirts and pants to the office before they left. Connor knew it was new. They had forgotten to take one of the little tags off when they gave it to him. He acted like he didn't see Jamie pull it off. It was real nice of them to get him some clothes. He didn't know how he was going to pay them back, but he would. Every penny of it, even if it took him a hundred years.

The bandages at his back itched and he was getting really tired now. The warm car was making him feel too good and he tried hard to fight it. He had to see to his momma and Dr. Damon hadn't said he could stay in the house with her. He just said his momma was staying until she was better. When they pulled up in front of the big house, Connor could only stare at it. It took him a couple of seconds to realize that one of the other men was picking him up out of the car.

"Put me down. I can walk. I ain't no baby." He tried to struggle to get down, but this man, he thought someone said he was Byron, just tightened his hold.

"No, you're not a baby, but you're back is bleeding again and it's wet out here. We forgot to get you shoes. I know you're not stupid enough to believe we just had clothes lying around waiting for you so tell me what size shoes you wear and I'll go get them. My wife and I are going to get some supplies for Damon and it'll be no problem to pick you up a couple of things too."

"I don't know. My momma buys them. But the ones I had on are good still. I can't afford to pay you all back if you keep buying stuff we don't need. As soon as my momma is all right, we gotta get going again."

"That's really good of you, son, but let me tell you something, all right? Our mom taught us to be kind to our neighbors and to help those in need. You want to pay us back, then here's what you do. You get a little older and when you find someone who needs something just like you and your momma do now, you pay if forward. Help them for us, all right? That'll mean more to us than you thinking you have to pay us for helping you."

Connor nodded. He looked at the men and women who had come out in the cold to help him and his momma. Not one of them had said no to a thing they'd been asked to do. He had more clothes right now than he had in the last three years that these strangers had given him. His momma was getting help and so was he. And no one had yelled at him, hit him, or made him feel stupid or dumb either.

"Mister, thank you. I'll make sure I help somebody someday. I promise I'll pay it forward like you asked me to. I'll make sure my momma does too. I think my shoe is a two if you still want to get me some."

Connor ended up going with them to Wal-Mart. Damon had said he would be all right for a little while longer, but to make sure his back was kept dry. He was wide awake now. He'd never been in a Wal-Mart before and was excited to see one of the places the commercials on television talked about. But the stop at the fast food place would be his favorite.

When they went through the drive-thru, it took Connor a few seconds to realize they had been talking to him about what he wanted. He was sitting in the back seat of the really nice car when Byron's pretty wife Taylor turned around and asked him what he wanted. He had no idea. This was another place he'd never been before and just looked at the pretty pictures on the menu.

"Do you think I could have a shake and some fries? I saw them once on a commercial and that lady seemed to really like them. I've never had a burger before but one my momma fixed. Are they the same as here?"

He ended up with two burgers, a large fry, a chocolate shake, and a cola. He was just finishing off the last bite when they pulled into the brightly lit parking lot. A full belly and a warm car made him a little tired, but he had to come help them pick out a few things for his momma to wear when she was better, Dane had said. He couldn't let her down. Connor didn't object when they got a cart and asked if he wanted to ride in the front. He was too tired to point out that he could walk.

By the time they were through the checkout and putting the hundreds of bags in the back of the car, he was dizzy with exhaustion. When he got in the back seat, he even let Byron buckle him in and make sure the seat belt was tight. They were pulling out of the parking space when his head fell to the side and he was out.

Connor never remembered the ride to the house where his mother was being operated on in the office in the basement. He didn't stir when Byron picked him up and carried him in the house and up the stairs. He didn't fight when Morgan stripped him down to his underpants and put his new pajamas on him and pulled the covers over his little body. Connor barely moved all night long. Warmth and security was something he'd not had much of in the last three years. And for the first time in all that time, he slept the night through.

Chapter 3

Damon was sitting at the kitchen table when Connor came downstairs. He smiled at the little boy. He had on the ugliest jammies he'd ever seen and he had seen a lot of them being a doctor.

"I done stripped the bed down and if you show me the washer, I can get them cleaned up. I'm sorry about the blood, but I think it'll wash out. I'd like to see my momma before you have me do any chores, please. I can cook breakfast for you too."

Damon felt the anger surge through him again. He had spent the better part of five hours stitching and repairing the woman downstairs and an hour fixing Connor's wounds while he slept. He'd almost not had to sedate Connor he'd been so tired last night. Damon had called Cait and had her come in and take pictures of the bruises and other injuries that they both had.

Connor's mother had four broken ribs and two cracked. Her throat was bruised and the hand prints were a perfect circle around her neck. Her left breast had been so badly bruised that Damon had had to step back from the table and take several deep breaths before he could continue working. Tansy, his nurse, had not said a word, but he could feel her anger too. Charlotte's left leg had been cut up badly and he wondered how she had managed to walk at all. It looked to Cait like a knife had been used with the blunt end against her.

And Connor wanted to know what chores he needed done. Damon took a sip of his coffee before he felt he could answer without screaming out the injustice of it all.

"Your momma is still asleep. I gave her something to help her rest and it'll be a couple of days before I want her to wake up. She'll need it to heal. You were right, she was in a great deal of pain. I'll take you down to see her in a bit. As for chores for you, I have a woman who comes in and does all that. I could do it myself, but I have to work every day and she likes working for me. I do need something from you. You remember Morgan? She has two little boys who are making her crazy to go to the zoo. She said if you went with her and helped her keep an eye on them, she'd buy you lunch. Morgan is very protective of her sons and for her to ask you to help is a big deal. None of us have ever been asked to watch them yet."

Which was all true. He told Connor he'd not lie to him and he promised he wouldn't. At least not right out. Yes, Morgan needed to take the boys to the zoo, and yes, she said she would buy Connor's lunch, and no, none of them had ever watched the boys, at least not without Morgan or Nicky close at hand.

"Okay. I'll help her. Mr. Byron told me that I should keep track of the help you guys give me and my momma and someday when I'm bigger I can pay it forward. I like that idea. I'm gonna pay you for your doctoring of my momma and me, though. That's different than helping with some clothes and stuff. Doctor College is hard and takes a lot of money."

"You pay me back the way you're paying the others. My education was paid for a long time ago. I was going to fix us some breakfast. If you want to go up and take a shower, it'll be done when you come back down. Byron said he bought you some stuff to use. The room you were in, that'll be yours until you and your mom are well enough to leave. And Connor, that'll be at least a month or so. So you make that room yours in any way you want. The bathroom in there is yours too."

Connor stared at him for several long moments, then he got up to go. Halfway to the door leading out of the kitchen, he turned back to Damon. There was a strange look on his face.

"I don't know how to make it my room, Dr. Damon. I ain't never...I've never had one before. Mr. O put me in the basement at night time and it was just a hard floor and a blanket. Momma would be down there with me most nights 'cause she tried to kill him a couple of times and he was afraid of her. I like the room, though. It's really nice."

He took off before Damon could form a word around the lump in his throat. Turning to the sink to fight tears for the kid, Damon knew as soon as he found that piece of worthless trash Mr. O, he was going to beat the living shit out of him then find a tree and hang him in it. Then maybe he'd shoot him in the twig and berries, as Pi liked to call the male anatomy. Twice.

Damon had French toast and bacon ready when Connor came back downstairs. He wanted to laugh, but didn't. The same ugly design on the jammies was on the

25

front of his shirt. What on earth possessed Byron to buy something with a large slice of cheese with pants and a tie on it was beyond him. When he commented on it, Connor explained it was a sponge, not cheese. Then he sang him the song Connor told him that a kid at his class had taught him. Damon caught himself humming the silly tune all day.

Morgan picked Connor up at ten just as they were coming up from looking in on his mom. She said she had to get the boys some new shoes before they could go. She and Connor were talking about what style he liked as they went to the car. Damon went back down to the woman.

She was pretty, he thought. It was kind of hard to tell with the bruises on her face. Her eye color was difficult to tell as well as both her eyes were bloodshot, but he thought they were blue. Her hair was blond and about medium length. It looked as if she had cut it herself or Connor had. Tansy said that women did that sort of thing to change their appearance to hide out. He thought she was probably right. She, like Connor, was undernourished and dehydrated, but with the IV he had running, she would be better soon. He'd made sure Connor drank two glasses of juice at breakfast. Her eyes were just fluttering open when Tansy walked in the door to the basement offices.

"Don't try to talk too much, miss. This is Tansy, my nurse. She'll be staying with you until I return. I have rounds to make and I can't miss them. Your son is with my sister-in-law, Morgan. She has two of her own so she knows how to handle kids. She knows to keep him safe. Are you in any pain?"

"No, not much. Connor safe? I want to see him. Please?" He knew she was in more pain than she was saying. Every move she made caused her to grimace and stiffen.

"We're going to move you up to one of the bedrooms as soon as I return. Once up there, you'll have to rest up. I'm concerned about the little bit of fluid in your lungs and I don't want it to go into something more before your ribs are healed. In a couple of days, I'll get you up and about then we'll see about getting you going up and down stairs."

"Connor. I want Connor." He smiled at her tone. It left no doubt that if she had been able, she would have gotten up and demanded a little more forcefully to see her son.

"He's not here. He and my nephews are at the zoo with Morgan. I'm sure he'll tell you all about it when they get back. You rest now. I'll be back soon."

~~~

"You should have seen it, Momma. I thought Morgan was going to pee in her pants. That kid just jumped out of the cart he was in and right into the door. If I hadn't been there, he might have bashed his whole skull in to his brain. She musta thanked me a thousand times. It was starting to get on my last nerve. And she let me spend as much as I wanted in the store as a reward. I didn't get nothing but a poster. Damon said I could decorate the room I'm staying in like I wanted. I really liked the zoo. How you feeling?"

Connor had come in as soon as he'd gotten home. That had been almost an hour ago. Charlie had heard the child jumping out of the stroller story three times now and the number of times he'd been thanked had tripled.

Smiling through the pain had never felt so good. Damon and Tansy had moved her up to this room at around one and she had been dozing until four when Connor quietly came in.

The room was beautiful. The bed she was in was a king-sized four poster with a canopy. The blanket and comforter were dark blood red velvet and so soft under her fingers that she couldn't resist running them over it. The lace of the canopy alone probably cost more than her entire wardrobe at the Ormond house, including the thing they were stored in. The matching dresser and tallboy were dark like the wood of the bed, and the same lace was in the curtains at the windows. There were four of those, two on each side of the bed, and sunlight filtered through the room. The walls were a dark paneling and she doubted it was anything but real wood and not the kind that came in sheets to look like wood. There was even a fireplace that had fake logs in it and was burning brightly in the warm room. Tansy had told her that when they took the catheter out, she had her own bathroom and there was a nice deep tub and a shower big enough to house the entire bunch of those Grant boys.

"So you you're being really careful, aren't you? I know you're having a good time, but we can't get too attached, Connor. If Anthony finds us, we'll have to get out quick. These people have been nice to us, but you know what he is and those people stick together."

Everytime she and Connor had gotten away, they were brought right back to him. No one would listen to them. He had them eating out of the palm of his hand. The one time they had gotten the lady at the shelter to listen, she had ended up dead the following week. Accident, they had said. Well, she knew better.

"I'm being careful. Momma, I really like it here. Damon and his brothers are real big. Maybe they can whop him some so he'll leave us alone. He whops on people and they leave him alone."

"What if they can't beat him, honey? Do you want something to happen to your new friends? I don't. Dr. Grant has been very kind to us. But they also seem like they obey the law. I don't want to make them have to choose between us or him. As soon as I'm able, we'll move on. Don't get any more attached to these people than you already are, baby."

Connor left her soon after that. He had grown quiet when she told him they had to leave again. But what choice did they have? Anthony had money and he had a badge. Two things people like her couldn't win against.

It was nearly six o'clock when Damon came into the room. He was upset about something, but he didn't take it out on her. She didn't ask him what it was. She, too, had to pull back from these nice people. And Damon Grant was too handsome and too nice for her to get attached too. Especially under the circumstances.

Charlie knew what she was. She was what her momma called a slut. She'd had Connor when she'd just been seventeen. Connor's daddy had taken advantage of Charlie after getting her drugged up on something. She didn't remember a thing other than waking up with sticky blood on her thighs.

He'd told everyone at school he'd had her. Told them all what a lousy lay she'd been too. She couldn't deny or confirm anything until three months later when the doctor told her momma Charlie was expecting. Of course she'd kicked Charlie out. Her being a Christian lady and all, she couldn't have a slut daughter around when the ladies of the Church came by.

It took her a while, but Charlie had gotten her education and even went on to take nursing classes after Connor had been born. Mostly it had been paid for by the government, but she still had to work. Babysitting was expensive and so were diapers and formula.

Then one night while working at the hospital in Tulsa, Anthony Ormond had come in with a suspect. While she stitched up the man's arm that he claimed the officer had done after he'd gotten into the cruiser, Ormond asked her out and she had refused. He was handsome in an "I know I'm good-looking" sort of way. But Charlie had a plan and it didn't involve a man she didn't trust. Over the next several days, he kept showing up at her job. Then at her home while she was there and sometimes while she wasn't. The last straw had come when he had taken Connor out of the daycare center he'd been in and brought him to his house.

"You stay away from me, Officer. I've told you several times I want nothing to do with you. I have a son, my son, and we are going to make it on our own. You come around again and I'll report you to your boss."

The next night, she got a ticket for speeding. She hadn't even driven her car to work. The officer, Officer Crews, had showed up at her work and told her that he'd clocked her going ninety in a thirty-five. When she tried to explain that her car was in the shop and had been for over a week, he took the ticket back and put the date for the previous week on it. The next afternoon, she sold the car.

It took all day at the court house to try to get someone to listen to her and finally, she had ended up paying the ticket and letting it go. She couldn't afford to miss any more work over it. Three days later, she was arrested.

She was caught shoplifting, the arresting officer said. When she asked him from where and when, he didn't say a thing, only put her in the back of his cruiser and took her down town. That's when Anthony explained to her how things were going to go from then on.

"I'm going to go get that brat of yours and when we come back, you are gonna pack up your shit and move in my house. Then when I feel you've learned your lesson, I'll take you down to the court house and we'll marry. I don't wanna hear no more bitching about how you're going to make it on your own. I decided your mine and that's all there is to it. Understand me?"

"Why are you doing this? I don't even like you. I want you to leave us alone or I swear to—" That was the first time he'd hit her. His fist had come out so fast and connected with her jaw that she was on the floor and bleeding before she could react. The next time he hit her was the same evening when the evening sitter wouldn't give Connor to him. He'd beaten her so badly that time that she spent time in the hospital.

She'd called her best friend Jorden and had her bring Connor in and they had run. They made it all the way across the state before he found them. Another four days in the hospital with two broken ribs and a broken arm.

With him holding Connor hostage, she had no choice. She moved in.

Every time he took her to the court house to marry, she would have such a fit that he would bring her back without it happening. It cost her. Every time she denied him, he would beat her. Sometimes so badly that she would spend days, even weeks, in the hospital. The good thing was that he didn't believe in premarital sex. She didn't understand his logic in that. He'd beat her senseless then he tell her it was a sin to have sex without the benefit of marriage. She was fine with that. Then he'd hit Connor.

Connor had just turned five. He wanted to go to school and when Anthony had told him no, Connor had told him to go to hell. He had backhanded the little boy.

"You'll have respect for your provider, boy. I don't have to have you as part of the deal. You'll listen to me or feel my belt on your back 'til you bleed. You should feel honored that I'm willing to take something like you into my house and raise."

Charlie came at him with a skillet. She'd hit him several times that day, mostly in the head, before he left the house screaming that she was nuts. No police came to see what the screaming was about, but then she wasn't surprised. They never even came when she called them to help her. She and Connor left with only their clothes on their backs. It had taken him eight days to find them. She'd heard that he had hired some psychic woman to find them, but that she'd been no help. Thank goodness. That had been five months ago. Then four days ago, she and Connor gotten away again.

It had taken some work and nerves of steel to do it. They didn't have any money and knew that in order to get any, they'd have to figure out a way to get into his locked bedroom while he was gone. The padlock on the door was bad enough, but the bars on the windows were nearly impossible to overcome. The plan was to get Connor inside in the morning and then out again that night. It had to be him because Charlie was too important to the daily activities around the house to be missing that long. When Anthony went to the bathroom to shower, Connor slid in the crack of the door and under the bed. Once he was locked in for the day, then there was no getting him out again until Anthony came home and opened the lock again. And that terrified Charlie worst of all.

They had nearly gotten caught when Anthony had asked where her brat was and Charlie didn't know. He had slapped her and when Connor had heard it, he had made a noise. Charlie grabbed Anthony to keep him from going to look for Connor and that was when he'd beaten her as badly as he had. It was another day before they could leave. Charlie was in so much pain and then Anthony had beaten Connor when he had burnt the toast for his dinner. The belt had always scared Connor and he knew it.

The morning after that, they walked to the next town and then got on a bus. The driver, another woman, had helped them get on and had even let them stay on the bus and got food for them when they made stops. That was probably the only reason they'd made it this far. No one had ever seen the two of them but the cross-country drivers.

Chapter 4

Damon had fixed dinner for him and Connor about an hour ago and the little boy was so quiet that Damon knew something was wrong. He'd tried asking, but Connor just shrugged his tiny shoulders and continued to play with his food. As soon as the meal was over, he went to his room and closed the door, not even going to see his momma.

Damon was fussing in her room trying to figure out how to ask Charlie about her son. He didn't want to alarm her with anything. Damon was sure that little boys had moods just like adults, but he was concerned. Finally, he sat on the chair next to the bed and told her about her injuries.

"You will be able to get up in the morning. I want to have Tansy here just in case you get a little dizzy and I'll need help getting you back to bed. You're such a little thing I could carry you, but I don't want to cause you any undue harm. The catheter will come out too if you get along well enough. Do you have any questions?"

"I'd like to get moving again. Connor told me he explained what was going on in our personal lives. He shouldn't have said anything and I'm sorry for that. As soon as possible, we'll leave. If you could give me a total of what we owe you, I'll give you as much as we can and I'll send you the rest if we make it out of here."

Damon wanted to tell her she wasn't going anywhere, but for some reason knew that she would dig in her heels and leave in spite of him. He had to figure out a tactful way of letting her know she could depend on him, all of them.

"Miss Kirkpatrick, you're welcome here for as long as you need to be. No one knows where you are and you are certainly no trouble. My family loves Connor already, especially Morgan. I think she'd take him in a heartbeat if she thought—"

"He's mine! No one is taking him from me, you hear me? He's my son and I'm going to take him when I leave. And no one is going to hit him again either, not so long as I have breath in my body."

Damon let her rant. He knew that she wasn't lashing out at him but at the man who had hurt them. When she wiped at the tears on her cheeks for the second time, he got up and handed her a box of tissues that were on the end table next to the bed. He didn't say a word, but returned to his chair while she blew her nose.

"I haven't a clue what this man has over you, if anything, but I do not work like that. I have never hit anyone except my brothers and believe me, they hit back. Connor and you are welcome here. I was only saying that Morgan loves him because he saved one of her sons a hard bump to the head and probably several stitches. She said she had never spent a more enjoyable afternoon with anyone as she had with him. He was polite and very generous with his time and patience with the boys. You are raising a very fine boy there. As for what he shared with us, that is something that—"

"I'm not going to give you anything more on our personal—"

"That's quite enough! You have been snarling at me since you woke up. I am not this other man. I am Damon Grant. And if you continue to piss me off, I will not kiss you."

He stalked out of the room. Damon wasn't sure which of them was more shocked, her or him. He didn't have any idea why he'd said he was going to kiss her and until that very moment, he hadn't had any clue he had even wanted to. But now that the thought had entered his head, he wondered what it would be like. He walked down to the other bedroom that Connor was in and knocked on the door lightly. At his quiet, "it's your house," he went in.

Connor was standing on a chair trying to tape up the poster he'd gotten today. Damon felt his heart leap to his throat, but didn't move to pull him down. Instead, he walked up behind him and held the poster in place with his longer reach. The tape Connor had in his hand was wadded up and stuck to everything but his fingers. In frustration, he threw it in the trash.

"Shouldn't hang it anyway. I'll just have to leave it when I go. Don't know why I even wanted the stupid thing. Just got it 'cause there was nothing else there to buy and she wanted me to have something." He flopped down on the bed and left Damon standing there holding the poster.

"Wait right here and I'll be right back." He went to his office and found some tacks. He was nearly back to the room when he remembered something else, headed back to his room, and picked it up. Connor was wiping at his face when he walked in. Damon went to the desk and laid the tacks and book on the table, giving Connor space.

"Damon, you think I could get something to drink? I'll drink it in the kitchen and be real careful with it. I won't make a mess." Smiling, Damon thought he was a great kid.

"Sure, but if you wait a second, we'll hang this poster up and then I'll join you. I think I could use some tea myself. You want it over here or closer to the desk? I think this was a good choice, by the way. Having a poster with all the animals on it gives you lots of memories of them instead of one with just the pandas on it, I think."

He was quiet for a long time, so long that Damon turned to look at him. Connor was staring at the closet with his clothes hanging there. Damon thought he looked sad and a bit lonely.

"I've never had stuff before. Momma tried, but that bastard, he'd tear it up 'cause it was mine. He didn't want me, just Momma. He told her that if I were to die on the street, he'd not shed a tear, but be happy. She cried for so long that I didn't think she'd ever quit. I don't want to go, Damon. But Momma said that if we stayed, you all might get hurt. He hurt her friend when we tried to get away before. Momma said that money and a badge is hard to fight. I guess she's right, huh?"

"Sometimes. But Connor, I'm not going to let anything happen to you or your mom. I made you a promise and I intend to keep it. You stick with me, kid, and we'll make you safe. You just have to trust me. I know that's hard, but you can."

It took them another thirty minutes to hang the poster. They hung it in four different places before they found one that was perfect. Damon decided that he was going to take the kid to get more things to put in his room. And he was going to have someone come in and set him up with a computer and some video games. He'd have to have Jacob or little James come over and help with that. Damon decided to get some things for Charlie too. And maybe he'd kiss her anyway.

~~~

Charlie was awake when Damon brought in her breakfast. It wasn't clear liquids anymore, but a bowl of oatmeal and toast. There was a large glass of juice and some fresh fruit, strawberries too. She looked up at him in surprise.

"I didn't cook this. My sister-in-law Ronnie came by and wanted to borrow the truck so while I cleaned out the firewood and swept it out for her, she made breakfast for us. Connor is on his second bowl. I wonder where he puts it all."

"It's lovely. I like oatmeal. And strawberries are my favorite fruit. Is Connor giving you any trouble?"

"No. I wish he would give me something to complain about. He's great. If you don't mind, it'll be me getting you up. Tansy had to go to her sister's last night and she won't be coming back until tomorrow."

She didn't understand what he wanted to complain about, but let it go. He went out of the room and when he returned, he had an arm load of towels and a bag. She flushed when she read the name on the bright pink bag.

"Cait and my mom went shopping yesterday and picked you up a few things. I didn't look inside, but from your embarrassment you know what's inside. There are also some pants and a shirt for you. They guessed on the sizes, but they seem to look all right all the time so it can't be too bad."

"Thank you, but I have some clothes of my—" She stopped when he raised his hand. He didn't look mad really just...she guessed frustrated with her. She smiled to herself. He didn't look like a man who had many people tell him no and probably even less of them told him they didn't need his help.

"As soon as you're finished, I'll take out the catheter. Then we'll see how well you do standing up. If you don't keel over, I'll let you take a quick shower, but I'm standing outside and the door will be opened. I'd have Ronnie come up and do it, but I'd still have to be close. It's not that I don't think she could do it, but I'd worry and have to be here anyway. Besides, Connor is charming her little girl."

When he cleared away her tray, she felt acutely aware of the man and not the doctor when he pulled out the needle to remove the fluid in the ball of the catheter. He never made a sound or touched her in any way but a professional one, yet she still felt her body stirring. She was so glad when he stepped away and went into the bath to dispose of the equipment and to turn on the water. All she could think about was the threatened kiss from last night.

"Okay, Charlie, put your arms around my neck and then when you're ready, we'll stand together. Don't try anything more than just standing for now and don't let me go until I tell you, all right?" She nodded.

With heart pounding, she stood up. Damon did most of the work. She didn't so much as stand as he lifted her to her feet. The room swayed just a little, but otherwise, she felt really good. She grinned up into his face and froze.

He was looking down at her with the fiercest look on his face. She wasn't afraid of him. On the contrary, she felt her breath catch and her pulse rate double. She was aware of his hands on her ribs and the heat that penetrated the thin gown she had on. Of his thigh pressed intimately between her legs and her fingers laced together behind his neck. When she licked her suddenly dry lips, his groan moved through her entire body.

"Charlie, I want to kiss you. But I don't want you to think I'm taking advantage of you and your situation. But tasting you right now is all I can think about. It's all I've thought about since last night."

His words were soft and gentle, but she could hear the need in them. It matched her own in both urgency and hunger. She moved toward his descending mouth and felt her eyes begin to close. When his mouth brushed over hers, she moaned at the contact.

"Momma! Momma, Miss Ronnie wants to know if I can go to the store with her and Marie. She wants to know if I got any halogens. You okay? You look all, I don't know, sort of red and all hot."

Damon hadn't pulled away from her, but held her. When she had tried to jerk away from him when she'd heard Connor bounding down the hall, he'd simply tightened his grip on her and held her firmly. She started to struggle, but he pressed his erection into her belly and she stopped.

His whispered, "Sorry, but it's not often I hold a beautiful woman in my arms," made her flush again.

"Well, do I? Momma, are you paying attention? You should go back to bed with Damon. I bet he could make you feel a whole lot better."

Damon laughed and she embarrassed more. Christ, what was wrong with her? She'd practically thrown the man to the bed and had her way with him and all he'd asked for was a kiss.

"No you don't have any allergies. Halogen is a gas. And I think you should stay here. You never know, I might need you for something." Yeah, like not leaving the room in case she lost her mind again and tried to kiss her doctor.

"I think you should let him go. You'll be all right with me. Cait is coming over in a little while to talk to you and it's sort of personal."

Yes, but would he be all right with her? "All right, Connor. But you listen to her. She's probably not used to children and I don't want you to upset her, all right? And you remember what I told you? You know it's right."

She saw his face drop. It hurt her to see him hurt, but they had no choice. He knew this as well as she did. They couldn't trust anyone. She felt the Damon's arms tighten around her.

As soon as she looked into his eyes, she realized that he knew. Connor must have said something to him about trust. She felt his withdrawal from her, not just physically but emotionally as well.

"Let's get you in the shower. I don't think you'll have time for a long one. I'm afraid that the hot water has been running for a while. There are girly soap things over your head. If you can't reach them, let me know now. Good. I'll be right out here."

He fled the room quicker than Connor had. She heard the steel in his voice. Trying not to think about what it meant, she washed her hair. The warm water felt good on her skin and the smell of the herbal shampoo and soft soap made her skin tingle and feel so soft. Lingering as long as she dared, she turned off the water and opened the shower door. Damon had his back to her with a towel in his hand.

"I've changed your bed linens, but if you want, I can take you downstairs. We don't want to overdo it. Yell when you're dressed and I'll be right there."

She fell in love with the pretty bra and panty sets. There was a beige set and a bright yellow set. Putting on the yellow, she felt pretty and a little sexy. She had never owned anything like it before. She'd always had to be thrifty when she and Connor had been buying things like under things. And when she lived at home, they had been white. The dark green blouse was a perfect fit. The long sleeves buttoned from the elbow to her wrist and the little buttons down the front were shaped like little clovers. The pants, a dark green denim and soft as butter, fit her like a glove and molded to her body like a second skin. She was just buttoning them up when Damon knocked at the door. She opened it and stepped out.

"I wasn't going to say anything, but I can't do it. You told him, didn't you? You told him not to trust us and that you were leaving as soon as you're better. Why would you do something like that to him? Why would you tell him not to trust us?"

"I don't know you. Why should I trust anything you do or say? I'm a woman on the run with an eight-year-old little boy and you think just because you're handsome and nice that I should blindly trust you?"

"I see. Me bringing you into my home, caring for you, and wanting to make sure you're healthy doesn't cut me any kind of slack with you. You would just rather lump all of us in the same category and be done with the whole lot of us. Is that it?"

"You don't know what we've been through. You have no idea what I've done to keep us safe, to keep Connor and me together."

"You're right. I don't. But then you never gave me or any of the rest of us the opportunity to find out either, did you? You closed the door on us the moment you opened your eyes. You should remember that I treated those wounds on your body, all of them. If that didn't give me the right to ask, then nothing did. But I didn't. I waited, hoping you would tell me on your own. But I guess that's never going to happen, is it, Ms. Kirkpatrick? I would appreciate it if when you leave, you would please let us all say good-bye to Connor. He's allowed us to grow quite fond of him."

With that, Damon walked out of the bedroom. He didn't slam the door shut, but closed it quietly, the sound of the knob clicking into place making her jump. Charlie thought she would have preferred him slamming it. Sitting down on the bed, she burst into tears. She had hurt him and her son. The only two men in the world who had done nothing but be kind to her.

Chapter 5

Anthony Ormond slammed down the phone. That bitch was lucky he was two hundred miles away or he'd have to go and teach her respect for the man and the badge. How dare she act as if he was responsible for Charlotte leaving. He looked up the next bus stop on the route Charlotte had taken.

It had been seven days now and nothing. He didn't have a clue, not even a single false lead. It was like she and the brat had simply disappeared. He dialed the next number, wondered how she had managed to get a bus ticket, and took the still ringing phone to his room and looked in his sock drawer.

"Son of a bitch! The little bitch robbed me. Fucking bitch is gonna pay for that. No more mister nice guy."

"Sir? This is Glassnode Bus Terminal. Is there something I can help you with?" Anthony grinned at the terror in the voice at the other end.

"Yes. I'm Officer Anthony Ormond. I'm looking for a woman and a br...kid who might have been on a bus that came into your station. Might have been within the last five days or less. She would have been hurt, the boy too."

Damn right they'd been hurt, he thought. He'd beaten her right good the morning she'd left and that was gonna be nothing like he gave her when he got her back. And that fucking brat was just gonna end. No need for him anymore. He was gonna end. He didn't want to raise any other man's fucking bastard anyway. He'd fuck Charlotte until she took his and then she'd be so busy with his that she'd be happy to have that brat gone.

"A woman and a little boy, you say? I'll have to check. We're a big station here and we have ten or so buses come in every three hours. Tell me what they look like. It might take me a couple of days to get back to you."

"Couple of days? I don't think so. You get back to me today, within the hour. This woman and her br...kid are wanted in a robbery. Stole about ten grand and I want it...the victim wants it back, now. The woman is tall, about five-nine. But skinny, long, dark blond hair. Blue eyes and sorta fat lips. The kid? Well, he's a kid. Don't know what to tell you there. Never really paid any never mind to him."

There had only been three hundred dollars missing, but he had discovered people were more apt to help if they thought larger sums of money had been involved. When he did a robbery call, he used the opposite logic. Then if the money was retrieved, he'd keep the difference. Sometimes more for his troubles. That's what insurance companies were for, weren't they?

"I'll do my best, officer, but like I said, we have a great many buses coming in here daily and I have at least seventy drivers. I'll let you know what I find, if anything. You have a nice day."

The stupid cocksucker didn't even take the information needed to call him back. He was just about to call him back when his radio squawked. Every fucking time he got to doing something, somebody would call him in.

"Officer Ormond speaking." He never knew who was going to be calling him so he had learned to be careful of his radio calls. The last time he'd gotten snippy with that bitch at dispatch, she'd told his boss. Bitch was probably sucking him off under the desk every day, that's the only reason he got his ass chewed out. It served her right that her tires had been slashed twice since them, he thought with a nasty grin.

"Aren't you supposed to be over at the school directing traffic? I gotta tell you this every day, Andy? Jesus H. Christ! Are you just that stupid? Haul your ass over there right now and get to it."

He hated being called "Andy." His name was Andrew Anthony Ormond and this cock sucking prick called him Andy every time he got the chance. He'd gone to his boss about it, but he'd said that David was just funning with him and if he ignored it then David would get tired of it and bother someone else. It wasn't worth getting in a tussle over. That had been three months ago. Anytime he wanted to move on to someone else was fine with Anthony.

"I'm headed there now. I got hung up on a traffic violation. Some woman wanted to argue her speed." That had been true, but it had happened over two hours ago.

"Sure it did. If you're still arguing her ticket after two hours and twelve minutes, why don't you just bring her in? Sounds like my wife anyway. Get a move on, Andy, right now. Kids can't cross the street without their pa-trol there to direct them."

Damn GPS and damn the way David said patrol like it was two separate words. As soon as he could, he was going to arrange for David Haddock to have a permanent accident. One that involved a great deal of pain for the man and whole lot more broken bones than the last time he'd had an "accident."

He was just pulling into the parking lot of the school when his cell went off. The number wasn't one he recognized, but he had given out his number a lot over the past week looking for his Charlotte. He answered with a short bark of his name.

"You still looking for the woman and her little boy? I think I saw them when I took the bus to my family's house to help to out. Got the gout, you see, and can't get around like they used to. I swear there are days when I think Gabby gets herself hurt just so I can come over there and see—"

"Where does your sister live? And when was this, exactly?" If he hadn't shut her off, no telling how much more he would have had to endure of her sister's gout problem. Anthony shuddered with disgust.

"Oh, she lives in that trailer park on London Street. Those things are so close together that I swear I can hear her neighbor's breathing at night. Then those dogs! Don't get me started on those dogs. Bark all night long, they do. Then there—"

"What city does your sister live in?" He enunciated each word and he could hear the bite of anger in his voice. At this point, he didn't fucking care.

"Cincinnati. Don't know why you'd want to know that. I thought you wanted to know about that woman and her little boy."

He counted to ten, then on to twenty. He tried to figure out when he'd lost the train of the conversation and couldn't find it. The woman had said she was visiting her family, that her sister had gotten hurt. He rubbed the point in his forehead just over his nose. The tension was growing and he mentally added another thing to beat Charlotte for when he found her. Tension was a killer.

"Where the fuck did you see the woman and kid? I don't want any kind of elaborate stories or sidetracks. Just tell me which bus you were on and where it was headed."

"There is no need for you to get rude, young man. Well, if I didn't think it was my Christian duty to keep a family together, I'd just hang up on you. You are a very nasty man. Washington D.C. And there's another thing I think—"

He disconnected the call. He didn't care how many other things she could think of at this point. He had a starting point and it was more than he'd had all week. Getting out of the cruiser, he walked up to the school just hoping some punk would give him lip. And if he or she did, then he'd see that someone left today with a fat one.

~~~

Cait walked up to the house and took a deep breath. She'd been back on duty for three weeks now and this was her first job that didn't involve pushing a pencil or typing

51

up some report. She missed her son and daughter, but needed to work too. If she had to stay at home much longer, Grant might have found her in the corner with her thumb in her mouth humming nursery rhymes to herself.

"He did it again, Captain Grant. I ain't gonna put up with his crap much more. Might have to take a stick to his hide if he does it or leave him. Can't say that he'd notice none unless his dinner was late."

Cait smiled. Yeah, this was a good reason to leave her children with a sitter. A woman half naked meeting her at the door with a shotgun.

"Mrs. Peabody, you need to put the gun down or I can't come in the house. I told you that the last time I was here. You need to stop waving it around before it goes off and you hurt someone."

"I'm gonna hurt that damned boy if he don't straighten up his act. Do you know how much he ran my phone bill up last month? Eight hundred and twelve dollars! That's more than I get working down at the IGA every two weeks. How am I supposed to pay that? He can't hold down a job and he damn sure ain't gonna share if he does."

"Just tell me what he did this time and let's see if I can help you out. You say he's not here? Where is he, do you know?" Cait was beginning to feel like she spent more time fixing family problems than anything. Didn't people want to get along? Now she sounded like one of those greeting card commercials.

"I think he's making that dope in his room. I can smell all kind of nasty stuff going on behind that door. And the people he has coming here all hours of the day and night.

It's making my nerves act up. He's trying to kill me so that he can live off my insurance and live here scot free."

Cait let Mrs. Peabody lead her down the hall. She was still a good four feet from it when Cait smelled it. Danny Peabody was dealing in meth. Cait grabbed Mrs. Peabody's shoulder, held her back, and motioned for her to go back to the kitchen. Cait followed, pulling out her cell as she went.

"Mrs. Peabody, is there anyone in that room? That you know of?" Her heart was pumping and she could feel the adrenaline running.

"No, he went out 'bout an hour ago. Won't be back until night, if he follows his usual pattern. You calling in the SWAT team, Captain Grant?"

With a wink at her, Cait identified herself to Commander Tucker. They'd both been promoted recently and were still having trouble remembering their new title.

"I'll need some back up at the Peabody place. I think little Danny has expanded his operations to meth. I'll wait here if you send in the big guys."

"Hot damn, wish I was with you. We've been trying to get that little turd for two years. I'm having…what the hell is her name again? Anyway, she's sending them out now. Oh, and your sister-in-law Dane called. Said for you to call her as soon as possible. She said that she has a feeling and that you'd understand. Why doesn't she just say that she had a premonition? Does she think I don't get her code speak?"

"I'll ask her, or maybe better yet, she can just call you and tell you what you want to know. Don't be a dork, Tuck, she's just covering her ass. Don't we all do it?"

"Yeah, I suppose so. But I tell you—Rachel! The girl who works for me is Rachel! Ha! I knew I'd get it sooner or later."

Cait hung up and called Dane. Dane had married Jamie a few months ago and they were expecting their first baby in a few months. She and Morgan were due about a month apart, Morgan to deliver first. Dane had just recently found out she was worth nearly eight billion dollars.

"Hey, it's Cait. Tucker said you had something for me. Anything on that shirt yet?"

"Cait, where did you get this stuff? Is it really from the woman and boy Damon is caring for? I know this man and he is worse than anyone thought. I don't suppose you got a name, did you?"

"No, not that I'm aware of. The only thing the kid has called him was the bastard. The woman has been too beat up for me to talk to. I'm actually going over there today after work. You want to come with me? I'm sure Damon won't mind. I think he's kind of sweet on the kid. Have you met Connor yet?"

Cait had heard the story from Morgan a couple of times how the kid, Connor, had leaped up and caught Daniel before he hit the open door with his forehead. And Ronnie and Margaret had spent the day with him this morning at the mall and the grocery store. She couldn't wait to talk to him again. At the scene with his mom, he'd been about half asleep and not saying much.

"Clear it with the woman and Damon and I'll go. Pi wants to take her some chicken soup and friendship. I swear that woman is driving me insane with this baby.

James is so laid back. Pi is like some sort of pregnancy police. I can't do anything without her having an absolute fit about it."

Cait knew about the pregnancy police. Her husband had been the same way. She heard the sirens coming and got off the phone with Dane. Over the next four hours, not only did they break up a fairly large meth lab, but Mrs. Peabody got her son out of the house once and for all.

Cait called Damon and had him ask Charlie if she and Dane could come over, but he said she was asleep. Connor was out with Byron buying a game system for the basement and Damon was getting ready to leave to deliver a baby at the hospital. He said he'd tell her who was coming and for them to come on in. Cait thought he sounded upset. And asked him about it.

"Nothing. She...Ms. Kirkpatrick told Connor...she doesn't trust me, Cait. Me! I don't think I've ever...not even as a new doctor has anyone not trusted me. She's going to run again too. Just as soon as she's able and she'll take that little boy with her. I wouldn't be surprised if they're gone already."

"I'm so sorry, Damon. Would you like for me to talk to her? Maybe we could get her into some woman's shelter or something until she's better. She might not be as safe there, but if she doesn't trust you then—"

"No. No, don't...I want her there. I...shit, Cait, what am I going to do? I've fallen in love with that kid and until today, I was kind of growing fond of Charlie too. No, that's not true. I am fond of her." There was a long pause then he said something that hurt her heart for him. "I guess

I'm not ever going to find anyone to love me. Boy did that sound childish. I'll talk to you later." And he hung up.

Cait stared at the paperwork in front of her and then picked up the phone. It was time to call in the big guns for this. If Damon found someone he liked, then she would move heaven and earth for him to have a chance at it.

"Margaret, it's Cait. I have a problem I think you're the only one who can help me with it. It's about Damon and Charlie."

An hour later, Cait hung up quite proud of herself. She knew that Margaret could talk to Charlie. If she couldn't, then she doubted the woman was worth it anyway. Cait called Dane to tell her she was on her way.

Chapter 6

Charlie woke up to the semi-dark room. She moved slowly and was startled to see an older woman sitting in the chair across from her. She was reading a book with the only source of light in the room. She was smiling at whatever it was she was reading. The woman looked over at Charlie as she turned the page.

"Good, you're awake. I'm Margaret Parker. How are you feeling, dear? You certainly look better. I told Ronnie that shirt would look good on someone with your complexion." The older woman stood, turned on the overhead light, and then sat back down.

"I...Damon—Dr. Grant left. I don't know when he'll be back. I think he was headed to the hospital." Charlie didn't have a clue where Damon was, but she didn't want to tell this lady that.

"Oh, he's delivering the Morton twins. Sally has nine children and two other sets of twins in that lot. Why she doesn't make that man of hers go get his balls cut is beyond me. No dear, I'm Damon's mother. I've come to talk to you."

Charlie looked at the door and then back to the woman. He called his mother on her? Margaret looked like she couldn't be any more than fifty at the most. There was no way she could be his mother. Then she thought something had happened to Connor.

"My son. I should go and find him. He was mad...he went to the store with someone this morning and I...I have to go and find him. Excuse me."

She started to rise and then sat back down. Hard. Dizziness swamped her and made her belly roll. She was trying to remember the last time she'd eaten when a small Chinese woman walked it with a big tray.

"Good, you eat. I bring you chicken soup. Missy Dane say it good for what hails you. Make no sense to me, but I bring it. Missy Margaret, I bring you bowl too. Boy, he eat five bowls. Good boy that. Washed dishes for me too."

Charlie looked at Margaret who just winked. She was still working on the Missy Dane part and then she realized that the boy who she was referring to was Connor. He'd eaten five bowls of soup? Before she could ask, the woman was out the door, leaving two huge bowls of thick soup on a tray with crackers and a carafe of iced tea and two glasses.

"That was Pi. She's a card. Most of the time it's easier to just nod at what she says than try to figure it out later. But she and I have been hanging out a lot now that Dane is pregnant so I think I'm getting used to her. She does need to grow on you for you to appreciate her."

Charlie thought she might be right. The soup smelled so good that her mouth watered for it. It was thick with broth and handmade noodles that were perfectly cut and tender. The bits of chicken were juicy and tender and the herbs tasted fresh and hearty. She finished off the whole bowl without stopping. She could see why Connor had eaten five bowls.

"I always find a bowl of soup makes you feel so much better, don't you think?" Margaret questioned as she wiped her mouth. "Would you like to go downstairs now? You have company. Cait and Dane are here and they'd like to ask you a few questions. Now don't get upset, it's not whatever is going through your mind. They've come to help you and Connor."

Charlie stood and didn't get too dizzy, but Margaret never left her side as she led her to the bathroom. She went to the bathroom and then brushed her teeth. By the time she walked out, she was tired again.

"I seem to get so tired so easily right now. I think I need to start moving around more to build up my strength again. Maybe walk up and down the stairs a few times a day."

Charlie needed to get out of here, out of this house and out of these people's lives. It wasn't that they were bad people, but they could run a person's life if one let them. Especially this one. Charlie just knew she had an addendum.

"No, you wait until Damon tells you to do that. You don't want to mess up all his hard work now, do you? He's a good man, my Damon. Why don't you like him?"

Charlie stopped on the stairs. She looked over at the woman who had her elbow and sputtered. *Didn't like Damon? Where on...*

"If he thinks sending you over here is going to make me change my mind, then you just wasted your time. We are leaving as soon as I'm able to take care of us. I appreciate everything he's done, but this is my fight and I will handle this on my own."

"I'm afraid it's not that easy, Ms Kirkpatrick. This man, I believe his name is Anthony Ormond, correct? He's killed before. Twice that I can tell, and maybe more. My name is Dane Grant. I'm Jamie's wife. I'm also a telepath."

~~~

Damon sat in his office and stared at the wall. He'd been here since Sally had her twins and he'd made sure she was all right. The proud parents had thanked him at least twenty times and he'd told them it was no problem that many back. They had trusted him to deliver their children and he had.

Charlie didn't trust him. No, that wasn't right. She didn't actually trust anyone. And she was making Connor feel the same way. He didn't understand someone not trusting him, he supposed. It had never in all his life been an issue. He had not liked a few people. Nicky's first wife had been a real bitch. Then there was the nurse he'd almost hired out of college. She'd turned out to be a mass murderer. Not really, but she had ended up killing a man over some drugs.

Connor was a joy to be around and he seemed to trust him. They'd been doing some things in Damon's yard. Yesterday they had winterized the deck and had taken in all the chair cushions. He'd let Connor use the leaf blower to blow all the fall leaves off the deck and around the smaller trees. He'd had a blast. Damon could still hear his laughter. He could tell sometimes that he expected Damon to scream at him or hit. There was never any need for that.

Connor was a great kid and so what if he'd spilled the trash on the ground? They had spent a fun ten minutes picking it up again.

Damon knew he should get home. He didn't know what time Cait and Dane where coming over, but he should be there at least part of the time. Pi was coming too, he remembered. He pulled his coat on and was just leaving the office when his cell rang. It was his house.

"Hello?" He could hear voices in the back ground, Pi's mostly. And then he heard his mother's. Shit. He wondered who had called her. Cait. Damn it! He moved to the stairs when he repeated his greeting.

"Damon? It's Connor Joshua Kirkpatrick. I'm the kid that's staying at your house right now. Can you come home? There are fifty women here and they're...they're crying. I don't like it. My momma's crying, your momma's crying, and even that fat lady that says she not fat but preggers, whatever the heck that means. She sure looks fat to me. You have to come here and make them stop."

Damon laughed to himself. The boy sounded absolutely panicky. He didn't blame him; he couldn't stand to hear a woman cry either. Especially his mom. He had an idea that Connor was having the same problems.

"Tell you what, kiddo. You meet me in the driveway when I pull up and you and I will leave them to their tears. We'll go over to one of my other brothers', how about Jamie's. His wife isn't there so it'll be woman free. Just let me talk to your mom to ask first."

"Ah, Damon, that'll be great. I'll give her the phone now. Sheesh, it's like sob city here. Here's my momma."

There was a shuffle of the phone and then a teary Charlie came on. Damon suddenly found himself leaning against the wall for support. She was crying and he wanted to go to her and comfort her, hold her, and tell her it would all be all right.

"Damon? Connor said you needed him for something. He said that you were picking him up. Are you not coming home?"

Home? Yes, he wanted to come home. He wanted to come home to where she was and be with her. He wanted to make a home with her. And he didn't have the slightest clue where that had come from. He cleared his throat twice before he trusted himself to speak.

"Yes, if it's okay with you, he and I are going over to Jamie's house. We won't be long, couple of hours. It sounds like...it sounds as if you're having a party. Is everything all right?"

She was quiet for so long Damon was afraid she wouldn't answer him. He nearly asked her again when she finally did. He held his breath.

"I'm not a nice person, am I? Don't answer that. I have...I should have told you at first that...would it be all right if you and I had a talk sometime? Maybe tonight after Connor goes to bed. I have to...Dane is here and she told me that he's coming. I want to...Damon, I don't know how to trust anyone. I've been making it on my own for a long time."

"It's all right, sweetheart. You and I will talk tonight. Can you call me and let me know when your cry party is over? Connor called me to rescue him, that's really why I'm taking him. I think he was a tad overwhelmed."

"Yes, he hates it when I cry. All right then. I'll let him come out to you when you call to say you're here. But not a moment before."

Damon wanted to tell her to come with them. To come with them and forget crying, but he knew enough about women to know that there were times that they needed to sob and cry and throw a fit. He just didn't want to be around one when they did. Twenty minutes later, he was helping Connor buckle in the car.

Jamie and Byron decided to meet at the pizza place. Nicky and Morgan were out and they came by too. When Spencer called to ask why the women were headed to Damon's house, he just told him not to ask and met them for pizza. Morgan left with the twins to go to Damon's house too. They called Devin and invited him to have an all-boys night of it. He showed up just as the pizzas were being served.

"Hey, you getting your house back after this? I understand that they're all there, including Pi. Can't bode well for your decorating skills. Ala bachelor is going to be no more, I bet," Jamie said as he tore out two slices of cheese pizza.

"They were crying. You should have seen it. I ain't never…I've never seen so many tissue boxes in my life. I had to empty the trash can in the living room twice before Damon came to get me." They all laughed at Connor's comment.

"Ah Damon, you never leave a man behind! Damn, man, that kid could be scarred for life. Think how much it's gonna cost you in therapy when you and Charlie get together. Good thing you have a good job."

No one said anything at Nicky's prediction. Damon wanted to beat him to a pulp. Connor looked confused and Byron couldn't stop laughing. Jamie was snickering, Devin was trying to cough his way out of it, and Spencer was stuffing a napkin in his mouth.

"Damon, you gonna get with my momma? She might not like that too much. She said men are pigs. I don't know what she means by that, but she says it like she means it. If you want to have her to like you, you should send her some flowers. She likes them."

"Really? What kind of flowers does your mom like, Connor? My wife loves roses and I know that Byron's wife likes daisies. I bet your mom is a violets type of woman." Nicky had been buying Morgan roses every week for the past four months.

"Nah, my momma said that she wanted a house someday so she can plant her some wild flowers. I picked her some one time when we was running, but they died. She liked them though."

"Connor, my man." Damon patted him on the back as he rose. "That's an excellent idea. I'll get your mother some wild flowers. Last man in pays, Devin. Sorry about your luck!"

They gathered up their coats and left soon after Devin paid the bill. Damon had a lot to think about, but he did stop at the store. He bought three bunches of flowers and a box of chocolates that Connor said his momma liked. He also picked up a box of condoms. He was a little embarrassed that he had no idea there were so many different kinds. So while Connor was looking for the perfect card for his mom, Damon read the labels. He ended up with two different kinds. They were pulling in the drive just as Pi and Dane were leaving.

"She okay? You guys scared poor Connor out of his manhood, you know? Couldn't you have waited until he was dating or something?"

Dane kissed him on the cheek and got in the car. Pi hugged him and told him that pizza was going to kill him. He needed to eat more Chinese food. He kissed her too. Connor had fallen asleep on the ride back and he lifted him to carry him in the house. Charlie was there waiting when he got to the door.

"I'll just take him up if you want to get him ready," Damon said as he shifted the boy to his other shoulder. "I got a call from the hospital on the way here. It won't take a minute. He had dinner by the way."

Damon went to his office and took the call from Tansy. Her sister had been admitted to the hospital and she wouldn't be in next week. Tansy's sister had been fighting cancer for several years now and she thought this was the end. He told her not to worry, but to keep him informed. He was just coming out of the office when Charlie came down the stairs.

Chapter 7

Charlie tucked Connor under the blankets and picked up his dirty clothes. She dropped them into the hamper when she noticed the bag lying next to them. There was a box of her favorite chocolates and a card. Connor had signed his name and put it on top. Inside the bag was another bag, well, two if you counted the double bagging. She was curious what else he'd bought and suddenly understood the reason it was bagged the way it was. There were two boxes of condoms, one ribbed the other "lubricated for her pleasure." Charlie carried it down stairs with her.

Damon was just coming out of his office when she got to the bottom stair. He looked upset and she slid the bag behind her. She didn't want to tease him if he'd get mad.

"Everything all right? You have to go back to the hospital? I hope it's not the twins. Margaret said you delivered a set tonight."

He didn't say anything, but walked to where she was. He was just a few inches from her when he reached up and smoothed the hair from her shoulder. She had not pulled it back up when she'd changed out of her dress clothes. When she started to pull it back up, he stopped her.

"Don't. I like it down. It's beautiful like this. You're beautiful like this. No, nothing is wrong with the twins or the mom. Tansy called. Her sister is in the hospital. She has cancer and Tansy is going to…Charlie, I'd really like to kiss you. Would it be all right if I did?"

She didn't answer. She pulled the bags out and handed them to him. She nearly burst out laughing when he blushed. Doctor Damon Grant was embarrassed. She decided to try and have fun with him.

"Were you buying these because you planned to get lucky or where you planning for my son to get lucky. They were in his bag. And if you were planning to get lucky, who's the girl?"

His grin was charming. It made him look so innocent that she wondered how long he'd been using that same look on unsuspecting women to get what he wanted. But the look in his eyes was not so much charming as it was rapacious.

"Charlie, if you don't want me to take you right here on the stairs, you'd better run. Now. And if you want me as badly as I do you, my bedroom is at the top of the stairs and to the left. The only door at that end. But know this, you aren't leaving that room until morning or we run out of protection if you go in there. I hope you go in there, but if you don't, then that's okay too."

"You'd be okay with me going down to my room, wouldn't you? You'd let me go and not say another word about it. Not make me feel guilty or hurt me, would you?"

"No. I'm not that sort of man. Don't get me wrong, I'll be disappointed. I want you. I want you in the worst way. But I don't want you so badly that I'll take you."

She stared up at him for several seconds and then turned on her heel and went up the stairs. He stood where he was. When she made a right, he didn't say a word but watched her. She turned back to him.

"I have to get my robe from this room. Why don't you lock up, Damon? That way you won't have to leave the room either."

She went down to her room and was just stepping through the doorway when she heard him "whoop." She was in his room first. More nervous than she'd ever been, she walked around.

It was a huge room. Bigger than any of the other bedrooms in the house, this one was twice the size as the one she slept in and nearly three times the size of Connor's, and they were all big rooms too. She looked around in wonder.

There was one wall that had nothing but shelves. In addition to books, there were large pottery pieces and small ones. She had heard from one of the women tonight that Byron was a potter and a famous artist. She wondered if any of the pieces were his. The framed photos fascinated her. She could see Damon as a child in a few of them. There were quite a few of all the men, now and as boys. There was a little girl in a few. She knew her to belong to Spencer and she could see her progression of growing up in the photos. The picture of the entire family in formal wear at Dane's and Jamie's wedding was nice and it showed a happy, loving family. Moving over, she looked at the book titles.

There were first editions of some great names, also paperbacks alongside of them. Damon seemed to have a much diversified reading habit. She liked that about him. She loved to read and didn't really have one author or genre when she read either.

The next wall was a bank of windows. The view from this side of the house must look out over the trees along the back of his yard. She couldn't see anything right now, but she would bet in the spring it was spectacular. The window seat in the little area was deep and the pillows and cushions looked used and well loved. There were two books on the little table next to it.

The fireplace was just there. She could see that it too was used and she thought what did the other women he brought here think of it? She felt herself get a little angry about that and then pulled back. What Damon did in this room was his business. She turned to leave when she noticed him standing in the doorway.

"I've never brought a woman to this house before. I'm not sure what you were thinking just now, but you looked pissed. I just wanted you to know that you're the only one who's ever been in this house. Aside from family."

"It's none of my business what you do or don't do in this room. And I wasn't pissed. I was...I was wondering if that pottery is your brother's, that's all."

She fussed with the pillow on the window seat as he came toward her. It was everything she could do not to cower. When his fingers ran down her, arm she felt the goose bumps rise on her skin and her nipples pucker.

"I would like for you to make it your business. I would like that very much, Charlie. Your skin is so soft and warm."

She took a shuddering breath and held it. When he lifted her hair from her neck and kissed her as he stood behind her, she closed her eyes and let her breath out slowly. His mouth was hot on her neck and his hands were so gentle. She wasn't sure how much longer she could stand if he kept touching her like this.

"Damon, I need to tell you…that feels so good. I need to tell you that…that I've never…well, I have but, Damon, if you don't stop for a minute I won't be able to tell you so…please, that was…do that again."

He had pressed her back against his chest and reached around and cupped her breasts. The bra she had on was another one that they had gotten her and this one was just a tiny scrap of lace and ribbons. The clasp in the front didn't stand a chance against Damon's nimble fingers. He had it open and his hands under her shirt in seconds.

He was gentle with her and she wanted more. It was then that she realized he was being careful of her still battered body. She covered his hands with hers and squeezed her breasts. She hoped he understood what she wanted and in the next breath, she knew he had.

"Untie the string for me, Charlie. Untie it and let your pants fall to the floor. I want to watch you undress."

She opened her eyes to see what she was doing and looked up. There was an oval mirror right in front of them and he was watching her. Charlie felt her pussy cream at the thought of him seeing her like this. When she fumbled with the string twice, he reached down and pulled it open for her. His fingers on her pale skin mesmerized her, the difference in their skin tones, and the size of his hands on her body. She pressed back more against him and moaned.

She was panting now as he slipped his long fingers into her pants and worked them down over her hips. When he got to her hips and the tiny thong she had on, he licked at the string and took it into his mouth. The entire time Damon was undressing her, he was watching her in the mirror.

When her pants were at her feet, he held his hand out so that she could steady herself while he slipped them over her feet. When he had them off, he ran his hands up and down her legs until she thought she'd scream. When he pulled her legs apart and moved in front of her, her legs trembled.

"I'm going to taste you, baby. I want to drink from you and have you come in my mouth. This room is far away from Connor's room so you let me hear you come, Charlie. I want you to scream out your release for me. All right?"

"Yes. Yes, please. Damon, I've never done this before. I...Connor's father was the only person I've slept with and I don't remember any of it. He took advantage of me. So I want you to know I have no experience in sex. So if you find me disappointing or lacking, that's why."

"Charlie. Shut up." He lowered his head to her mound and inhaled.

She felt herself gush more of her juices into her panties and tried to pull back from him. He cupped her ass cheeks and pulled her back with a growl that sent shivers down her body and into her pussy. When he pulled her panties down, his tongue entered her soft folds even while he took them off her feet. Then his hands pulled her tight against his mouth again. Over and over his tongue entered her and when he sucked her clit into his mouth and bit gently at it, she came. Her body spiraled out of control and she screamed out his name.

While her body was still trembling from the force of her first climax, Damon stood and picked her up. His mouth and chin were covered in her juices and she leaned up to kiss him. Never would she have thought something like her on his mouth would taste so good. He kissed her back, his tongue sweeping into her mouth and dueling with her own tongue.

~~~

When he laid her on the bed, he started to unbutton his shirt. She leaned up on her elbows to watch him. Her body was beautiful lying there open and bare to him. As she sat up to touch him, her hands running up his chest and under his shirt, he guided her hands to his chest then his ribs. Up and down his torso until she seemed to gain confidence. Once she had, he moved his hands to his side, he didn't touch her but watched, watched her as she explored his body.

"Take off your shirt for me. I want to see you, please. I want to touch you everywhere." Her voice was husky and deep; his cock tightened more, straining against his zipper.

He pulled the shirt off and let it slide to the floor. She pushed slightly against him and he took a step back as she stood up before him. Tentatively, she kissed his ribs, then his chest. When she moved up and licked at his puckered nipple, he moaned. She pulled back slightly and he cupped her head and brought her back to his nipple. When she licked him again, he tightened his grip in her hair.

"Please, Charlie. Don't stop, baby. Please, you're killing me."

His own voice was heavy with need. He wanted to toss her to the bed and take her hard and fast. Never had he wanted a woman so fiercely.

Sliding her hands down his abdomen, she stopped at the top of his pants and looked up at him. He nodded to her and put his hands over hers. Without taking his eyes off of hers, he moved them down his body to his cock. Slowly, he showed her what he wanted, how to touch him. Her moan made him ache with need.

Her fingers cupped him slightly then when he rocked against her hand, she wrapped her fingers around him and pressed back. His moan was deep; he felt it start at his toes and move out of his mouth. Lifting her chin up to kiss her, he watched, mesmerized when she licked her lips and then leaned in to lick his.

The snap on his pants came undone then he felt the zipper move down. The release of pressure on his cock felt good, but the feeling was short lived. Now it wanted relief more than ever. He wanted to be buried deep within her heat.

"Charlie...Christ, woman, if you don't touch me, I'm going to expire. I want to have this luscious body touching me. I want to feel your heat, your skin touching mine. Now, baby, I need you now."

Her hot hands were suddenly at the waistband of his briefs. He could feel the dampness of his pre-cum at the tip of his cock and when she wrapped her hand around him, he knew he was lost. Rocking hard into her fist, he cupped her breast and brought it to his mouth. Her nipple was hard and tight. Taking the tip into his mouth, he suckled it. When she pulled away and dropped back on the bed, he whimpered. Before he could protest, she was pulling his pants and briefs down. When she had them to his knees, she licked the drop of cum off him and then took him into her mouth.

"Christ!" He cupped her head. He wasn't sure if he wanted to pull her away or anchor her there. When she cupped his balls and rolled them in her palm, he felt his eyes roll to the back of his head. Stopping now was not an option.

Chapter 8

Charlie felt empowered when Damon groaned. Afraid that he would make her stop, she fisted her hand around his thick cock and ran her tongue down his length. He tasted hot and tangy. His skin felt velvety and hard under her hand. When his hand cupped over hers, she growled at him.

"Like this, baby. That's it. I'm so close, Charlie. You're going to make me come if you keep this up. And as much as I want to fuck you right now, I can't stop what you're doing to me."

He showed her how to touch him, how to cup him. Her pussy gushed at his words and when she tasted more of his thick cum on her tongue, she wanted it all. Wrapping her mouth around his cock, she fisted him tighter. When he started to pump harder in her mouth, touching the back of her throat, she took her free hand and touched her pussy.

"That's it, baby. Touch yourself. Let me see you pleasure that pretty pussy. Charlie, baby, I'm going to come. Pull away now if you don't want me to come in your mouth."

KATHI S. BARTON

His growl made her pull him deeper in her mouth. His cock touched the back of her throat with every surge forward. When his cum splashed against her tongue, she pinched her clit and moaned. Once, twice more she pulled and pinched until she came with him. He pumped into her, over and over her pussy tightened around her fingers as she swallowed every drop of him.

When he pulled away from her, she thought he was finished with her. She was startled when he scooped her up from the bed and pulled her body to his. His cock was still hard and she gasped when he dropped them both back down on the bed. She giggled when she realized that he had fallen because she hadn't taken his pants off all the way and he had become tangled in them.

"Woman! You trying to kill me? Never giggle when you're in bed with a man. You want me to have a complex?"

"You're much too sure of yourself to have a complex. Damon, please, I want to feel you inside of me. Please?"

Standing and stripping off his pants, he tossed them across the room. Then he leaned over and tore open the box of condoms that she had put on the bed when she came in. Opening the package with his mouth and taking out the protection, he rolled the latex over his cock and kneeled down over her.

"Charlie, I want you to ride me. I know it's been a while for you, so you set the pace for us. But I want you now. Feeling you take me into your heat, deep into your pussy, has me hungry for you. Coming in your mouth has only made me harder for you."

78

Damon rolled over her and settled on his back. She looked over at him and took a deep breath. His cock was huge and seeing it like this, hard and straining against his body, made her know that no matter how slow they took it, she was going to be sore tomorrow. Sitting up, she straddled his hips and reached out to grip him in her fist. He groaned again, sending shivers down her back and through her pussy to her clit. When he pulled her forward and his cock was beneath her, she rose up on her knees and watched as he guided his cock at her entrance.

"Slow, baby. Nice and slow. Christ, you're hot. And wet."

When she was seated just over him, his cock about halfway into her, he pulled her forward on his chest and kissed her. The kiss was deep and drugging. His tongue moved in and out of her mouth like she was dancing over his cock. When he gripped her hips and moved her up and down his shaft, she moaned. His cock touched her deep and abraded her inside, making her pussy clench him tight. She slid down deeper and then deeper still until he was fully inside of her. She sat up and rocked.

Damon's eyes watched her every move, his fingers dug deep into her hips. She knew there would be bruises, but she didn't care. He was inside of her. It took her a few tries, but once she got the rhythm, he reached up and put her hands on her breasts. With every downward motion, he surged up as she rode him. As he pulled and tugged on her nipples, she rode faster until he rolled her over onto her back and slammed into her. Wrapping her legs around his hips, she pulled his mouth to hers and nipped at him.

"Come for me, Charlie. I want to feel this hot pussy grip me. Take me with you, baby. Come. Come now."

Charlie's body responded to his command like it knew he owned it. When she cried out her release, she felt him stiffen then even through the condom, she could feel him empty into her. He pounded into her. When he dropped onto her, she felt drained and limp, sated, and relaxed. The last thing she remembered was him getting up and then quickly returning to her side. When he pulled her into his arms, she could do no more than let him do whatever he wanted. She drifted into a deep sleep, deeper than she had been able to manage in a long, long while.

Opening her eyes to a strange room gave her a start, then she remembered where she was. Stretching out, she realized two things at once. She was alone in the big bed and she was incredibly sore. Smiling at both ailments, she sat up. And found the note.

"Morning, Love. I have Connor with me. We have to go to the office for half a day. Then I need to meet with the tailor. We should be back around two or so. Call me whenever you want. Taylor called. She wants you to call her back.

Love, Damon and Connor

P.S. Dane dropped a bag of stuff off for you. It's in the bathroom. Connor made it difficult for me to say what I really wanted, but this room is ours now. Damon."

Charlie got up and moved to the bathroom. The large garden tub looked so inviting that she turned on the taps while she looked through the bag on the counter. She flushed at the assortment of personal things in it. In addition to the jeans and blouse, there were panty and bra sets like the ones from the day before, but also a set that left no doubt that it was made for a man in mind.

The black lace was decadent and sexy. She wondered if Damon would like them and smiled when she realized that she really wanted to see his face when he saw them on her. Holding up the bra, she looked at her reflection in the mirror and was shocked at what she saw. Her nipples were red and swollen, tender to the touch. There were tiny bite marks along her ribs and a set of bruises on her hips where he had held her. Her eyes looked heavy, but not from lack of sleep, more like she had been laid. Her mouth was also puffy and when she ran her fingers over her lips, she remembered the taste of Damon in her mouth, the feel of his cock pumping into her, and his cum sliding down her throat. Her body responded to the images going through her head and she felt her pussy heat and her juices flow. Good heavens, what would she be like if he were to touch her right now? She groaned at the thought. Dropping the sexy lace on the counter, she turned off the water and pulled the plug. She needed to get moving and a bath would only heat her up more. Turning on the shower to cold, she stepped in and squealed at the first touch. After getting cleaned up and dressed, she went to the kitchen and called Taylor.

"Are you okay from last night? We can be a bit overwhelming at first, I know. The first time I got together with all of them, I was terrified for a week. We are sort of your 'scared straight' for the Grant men. But don't you just love them?"

Charlie liked Taylor best. She seemed to have an air of not caring what anyone thought about her or what she said. She also was the bluntest in her assessment on how to deal with Anthony. Her ideal had been to hunt him down, cut off his dick, shove it up his ass, then tie him in a barn and set fire to it. Secretly, Charlie thought it a great idea too.

"No. Not really. Well, maybe just a little. I have a lot to think about, I guess. I'm still...I don't think that...Damon and I, we...shit!"

"Yeah, been there, done that. Christ, but they're good in bed, aren't they? Lethal almost. Anyway. I'm going to get a trim job, wanna come? It's my treat. Dane and the others are meeting us for lunch and I have a couple of things to get to. The office is going to be closed for the rest of the week for the holiday so I have lots of things to do while Byr is gone. He'll be back on Wednesday."

Charlie knew that Taylor had gotten a large insurance settlement when she helped uncover an insurance fraud with another firm. Taylor now worked for Nickolas and Devin as their receptionist, and her husband Byron was a famous potter and traveled a great deal.

"Um, sure. I don't drive. If you tell me where to meet you, I can call a cab. Connor is with Damon anyway. And I'd like to get trimmed up too."

Charlie and Connor had cut off her long hair when they'd left Ormond's house that morning. The color job was horrible, but it had allotted them some extra cover when running. She knew it wasn't great, but to have it cut nicely would be a big improvement when it grew back.

"I'll pick you up. Morgan is going to call Margaret and then there are the other four. I think Dane has to pick up her dress yet too. Did Damon ask you to go to the charity event with him? If he didn't, then you'll go with me. So, let's get you a dress for that while we're out. I'll be there in fifteen minutes." Then the line was dead.

That was another thing about Taylor she liked. Her "let's get it done and right fucking now." She was sure that her laid back husband took trips to get away from the little dynamo. Charlie was still smiling about it when the house phone rang. She didn't answer it, but let it go to voice mail. It was Damon.

"Hey, Charlie. Pick up the phone, baby, if your there. I want to talk to you about something. Charlie?"

"Hello? I'm here. I just got off the phone with Taylor. She is picking me up soon. Are you sure Connor isn't any bother?"

"Yes, I'm sure. He's a great kid. I forgot to ask you something last night. I think it was the sight of that luscious body that distracted me. I've been fighting a hard-on all morning and I can't wait to get back home and make love to you again. You're not too sore, are you?"

"No. Not too bad. I never…that was really nice. I…I almost took a bath, but I didn't think I'd ever get out just thinking about the things we did last night. The way your cock felt in my mouth."

He was quiet for so long she was nervous that she had said something wrong. But when he spoke again, she felt her whole body respond to his silky voice and his words. She was going to have to change again if he kept this up.

"I was going to be offended with the 'nice' comment, and then you had to mention you taking me into your mouth. Christ, I'm never going to make it through fittings.

I have to go and get—hello, Connor. I'm just talking to your mom."

Charlie burst out laughing at the abrupt subject change. When he growled at her, she knew he was going to make her pay for laughing and decided she was looking forward to it. She could hear her son in the background and knew that he was confused at Damon's behavior too.

"Okay, I'll ask her for us. Charlie, there's this thing this weekend. My mom has this huge event every year and it's formal. I'm going to pick up my tux today and have Connor fitted for one while I'm there. I want you both to be my dates for it. Will you?"

His date. She knew that they had slept together, but a date? With his family there too? She knew that this was going to be the turning point of their relationship, but she didn't feel panicky about it. She would need to talk to Connor first, but she knew that he liked Damon too.

"Yes. I mean, if you're sure. I'm not exactly the formalwear type. I don't even know how to buy a formal dress. Are you sure about this?" Okay, maybe a little panicky.

"Yes, I'm very sure. I guess you're going to be out with Taylor today. Have her help you. I'll call her about paying for the dress. I'm sorry it's last minute, but I'm sure she'll be able to help you out. Charlie? There's something I...I need to talk to you, baby. All right? Tonight. We'll talk tonight."

After talking with Connor and warning him to be careful and behave, she hung up. She wasn't thrilled about Damon paying for her dress, but knew that she couldn't afford anything near what he would be used to without his help. She was just putting the tea away when the doorbell rang. Taylor and Ronnie had come to get her.

It took Charlie twenty minutes to realize that she had been incredibly stupid. Well, it really hadn't taken that long, but long enough to realize that she needed to ask more specific questions when she went out with these women. The trim job hadn't had anything at all to do with her hair—at least not the hair on her head at any rate. They were getting their bodies trimmed, specifically their pussies waxed. Charlie had never felt so...well, she wasn't sure how to describe how she felt really. But she did go along with them. All she could think about was what Damon would think. And every time she did, she blushed. But the dress made it all worthwhile.

It was black and fit her like a glove. It was the first thing she tried on and the last. Dane wouldn't let her even look at anything else. The sleeveless confection molded to her breasts and was held in place by sheer willpower. She marveled at how sexy she looked in it, the way her breasts spilled over the top just enough to be feminine, yet decadent enough to look wanton. The slit up the sides would show off the thigh-high stockings she'd bought to go with it. The shoes were black as well with tiny, thin heels that added three inches to her already tall frame.

"Damon is going to swallow his tongue when he sees you in that. With your new haircut and a simple choker around your neck, you'll look like sex on a stick. You'll be lucky if you make it through the night without him finding a dark corner and fucking your brains out." Yeah, Taylor had a way with words.

They ended up meeting the men for dinner at their favorite restaurant. Dane had asked to speak to Charlie alone and when they went to the ladies room, Cait followed them. Charlie knew this couldn't be good.

Chapter 9

"Anthony is on his way here. I've figured out where he's at and where he's going. I have a few friends in the detective field that are keeping tabs on him for me. He's on his way to D.C. for some reason."

Cait looked so serious that Charlie wanted to cry. It had been such a wonderful day and now this man, Anthony, was intruding in on it. She wished she'd never seen the man.

"The bus Connor and I were on was headed that way. We only got off in Columbus because I couldn't ride anymore. We'd be there now instead of here if I hadn't been hurt so badly."

Charlie thought about these women coming to Damon's home that night and talking to her. They had all sobbed at what had happened to them and each of them had a similar story to tell about past men in their lives. She knew that she didn't have it as bad as the other women. Dane had been beaten and then disowned by her mother because she had a special gift that made her be able to touch people's lives in ways that would frighten others. Taylor had nearly been killed by her boss in addition to being hurt in a club by some idiot who had bitten her while she'd been tied up. Morgan had been kidnapped and raped repeatedly by a man who had simply wanted her. Then when she'd killed him to get away, she had spent five years in prison for it. Ronnie had had to kill her father because he was going to kill Devin. Cait had been shot several times by her partner and left for dead, then later had saved Meggie from certain death.

"Charlie, we need to tell them. The men, they have to know about Anthony and what he's capable of. We're going to need them to step up their security around us."

Dane had already told her this the other night and saying it again to her made her want to say no. But she was right. If nothing else, they'd need to be more careful too.

"All right. I should leave, though. I can't bring this to your family. This isn't right that I...he'll hurt you all to get to me. I don't know what I ever did to make him...oh, God, Connor is going to hate me. He loves Damon so much."

"Let's go back to our house and talk. But I don't think Damon is going to let you go. I believe he's in love with you too." With that, Dane left the bathroom.

Charlie looked at Cait. She didn't look too happy either. Charlie felt so horrible for what she had done to these people.

"Do you believe in fate, Charlie? I don't mean the fairy book kind where you find your one true love and you live happily ever after. I mean the way things just fall into place and it's just right. The reason I ask is because you fit with this family. I noticed the similarities the other day. Not one of us women has a mother, yet Margaret has acted like one to each of us as though she were meant for the job. We have no other family than who we bring with us. I didn't have anyone other than my Uncle Paddy and Aunt Dee and some bastard took them from me. Now I have Meggie, who I love as though she were my own, and Paddy. We each have had someone or something that has made us who we are and what we can become. Damon doesn't just love you. He doesn't just love Connor. He needs you. Both of you. I've never seen him so happy, as relaxed as he's been since you two have come into his life. We've all noticed it and thank you for it. All of us have depended on him, needed him for something or another. He saved my life when I was brought into the hospital. He's stitched me up and the others as well. When Morgan was pregnant with the twins, Damon even offered to marry her, not because he wanted her as his wife, but so that he could care for her when Nicky was being an ass. He has a huge heart and he's let you guys into it. Please don't hurt him by running again."

"I don't want him hurt. I...I love him too. I don't want anything to happen to him when Anthony comes to get me. What would I...I'd die if anything happened to him."

"Good girl. And nothing is going to happen to him or you and Connor. As of right now, you're a Grant. And Grants take care of their own."

~~~

Damon thought there was something wrong the minute Dane came back without Charlie. Then when Cait and Charlie came back, he knew there was. He started to rise and go to her, but her slight shake of her head stopped him. When she sat back down beside him, he took her hand and kissed it. Connor making a nasal noise brought laughter from the others at the table.

"Might as well get used to it, son," Byron said as he ruffled his hair. "They are going to be doing a lot of that, I'm thinking. Connor, why don't you come over to our house tonight? Taylor and I have a couple of questions to ask you about that new game we got today. She's a girl, you know, and she hates when things get…rough."

Everyone burst out laughing. There wasn't an adult at the table who didn't know that Taylor and Byron were into playing games during sex. That was how Byron had met his Taylor. She had come into one of his bondage clubs, Tightly Bound, and they had played together.

"Don't let him fool you, Connor. Bryon squeals like a little girl when I shoot him. I think he just wants you to show him how to shoot better," Taylor said with a wink.

"You people are weird. I really like you all, but you're all weird. Momma, can I go over? I'll be good and everything else." Connor looked at both him and his mother. Damon wanted to crow!

"Actually, we all need to go to our house. Jamie and I want to have you all over. We all have some things to discuss. If you don't mind, I'd like for you all to stay as well. Pi has been dying to cook for you all and this will be the perfect opportunity to let her have some fun," Dane said quietly.

"What's going on, Dane? Cait? Something's going on, isn't it? You can't just drop something like that on us and expect us to come along quietly. It'll drive poor Morgan here over the edge," Nicky said. His joke was strained.

"I think it's time that Connor and I...well, we've grown very fond of you all over the past few weeks and I think it's time we...we need to trust someone sometime and I can't think of anyone that I think we could trust more. The man who is...there's a man trying to get me and he's coming. I will understand if you want to bail out now. Connor and I will understand. We know what sort of man Anthony is and—"

"I know that I speak for the entire table when I say this. And Charlie, I say this with love and understanding too. Shut the fuck up and tell us," his mother snapped. "We aren't going anywhere and neither are you two."

No one moved. Their mother had never cursed at anyone...well, she had before, but not like this. Damon turned to Charlie and dropped to one knee before her. This was as good a time as any, he thought. Then realized this was perfect.

"Charlotte Kirkpatrick, will you do me the honor of becoming my wife? I want you and Connor to be my family. I love you both more than I've ever thought...I ever dreamed possible. I want to care for you both and keep you safe. I love you."

He trembled slightly when he pulled out the little box. He'd gotten it just today when he and Connor had been coming back from lunch. Having Connor there was wonderful and he knew he'd never forget the conversation he'd had with him for as long as he lived.

"Connor, I was wondering if I could talk to you about something. It's about you and your mom. Man to man sort of." He had babbled and had been afraid that he would screw this up.

"Sure, Damon. Can I have another burger first? I think that one was made on the skinny side, as my momma says. I have five dollars that Byron gave me for helping him hang one of his and Taylor's toys."

Damon nearly choked to death on his drink. He had thought he'd have to murder his brother when all Connor had helped hang was a pot rack in the kitchen. Connor had looked at him oddly for a few minutes.

"No, that's okay. Umm, let me pay, though. You're working for me today and I pay my men for their lunches. You go ahead, but don't get out of my sight."

When Connor returned with not one but three more burgers, Damon decided to see about investing in a large freezer for the house. Feeding this kid through his teenage years was going to be fun. He sat up in his chair while Connor polished the burgers off quickly.

"Connor? I wanted to ask you about staying with me. You and your mom, that is. I want to know if you want to stay with me."

"I thought we already were. Did Momma say we were moving again? I like staying with you. I like my room and all, but if Momma says we have to go then I gotta go with her. She needs me."

"Of course she does. No, what I meant was would you mind if I...you see, I really like your mom. She's wonderful and I love having...she's very special to me and I...that is to say that I..."

"Damon, why don't you just ask? We could get really old if you keep stopping and starting like that. You want to ask my momma to marry you, don't you?"

Out of the mouths of babes. "Yes. But I don't want to do it if you don't think I should. I understand that you and your mom are a package deal and I love the idea of you living with us too. I know I've not known you all that long, but I know that I want to spend the rest of my life with her."

"Yeah, okay, I guess. You and her gonna have kids too? I guess that'll be all right with me. When you gonna ask her?"

Damon had thought Connor had looked hurt, but then he'd asked about other children and all Damon could focus on then was seeing Charlie swollen with his child. He looked around the mall food court and saw a woman huge with child and could picture Charlie that way. It took him several times of clearing his throat before he could answer Connor.

"That would be something we'd all discuss. So, would you help me pick out a ring for her? I'd like to ask her this weekend at my mom's house. It's Thanksgiving, you know? I think she'd like knowing that you approved of me asking, don't you?"

So they'd spent a good two hours going from jewelry store to jewelry store to pick out the perfect ring. Connor knew she'd want something simple, though it had taken two very frustrated clerks and forty minutes of Damon wanting to wring his little neck to figure it out. Now here is was on bended knee with his family present, asking her.

"Momma, you gonna answer him? He sure took a long time picking out that thing. You gonna put it on or what? He knows that I come with you as a package deal, he said, so answer him."

Damon wasn't sure if he wanted to hug Connor or growl at him. The kid sure had a way of cutting to the heart of the matter. Damon took out the ring and picked up Charlie's hand. She was crying and he wished he'd done this with just the two of them. Maybe when he was buried deep inside of her. It was hard to say no to anything when in the throes of passion, he thought.

"Damon, are you sure? I mean, you don't even...what if we don't, you know what if we fight all the time and you hate me in a couple of weeks? I think you should think this through. I don't want to ruin—"

"If you finish that, I'm going to paddle you but good. I love you, Charlie. I think I have from the moment I first saw you. Please tell me yes. I'm an old man and this is killing me." He leaned up and whispered in her ear. "Besides, making up with you has its advantages too."

She blushed like he knew she would. For a mother of an eight-year-old, she was deliciously shy. He decided to talk to her about children too. He wanted everything with her. Starting with her having his last name.

"Yes, but only if you still want to after to—" He also decided that she talked entirely too much. Kissing her quiet had its advantages too. Damon thought he could get used to this. But soon he was being pulled away and Charlie was being welcomed to the family. He barely managed to get the ring on her finger before his brothers were all kissing her. He looked over at Connor.

"So, Connor, what do you say you and I get that room of yours fixed up more? I was thinking school too. Maybe we should get you enrolled starting Monday."

The kid actually growled at him.

Chapter 10

"I want you all to understand that if you change your mind about helping us, we'll both completely understand. I know that what I'm about to...Connor and I didn't ask for this, for any of this. He's my son and above everything else, I have to put him first."

She didn't want to tell them about this, but in order to know what she was dealing with, they needed to know everything. Including about Connor and her family. She was ashamed and when Connor came over and sat in her lap, he held him close to her.

"One night after the prom in my junior year of high school, Jorden, a girlfriend, and I went to a party. I didn't have a date to the prom, not that I could afford to go anyway, but the party was being given by someone I thought was a good friend. Allison had invited me specifically. There was alcohol there and older boys. Allison had an older brother and he had invited some of his friends too. His name was Brody, Brody Gibbons.

"He started flirting with me. I wasn't stupid enough to think he wanted anything more than to show off to his buddies, so I stayed away from him. He kept coming on to me until Jorden and I started hiding in the house until her dad came and got us. I had a sort of reputation of being somewhat cold, standoffish. I think he thought he'd prove how big of a man he was if he could have me.

"I don't remember much after that. I'd been drinking cola all night and Allison had brought me a glass into her room where Jorden and I had been hiding. I drank half and Jorden the other half. It wasn't...I ended up spending the night. I woke the next morning alone and naked in the bed, Brody next to me. He said that...he told me that the ice queen had been conquered and that I'd won him a bet. He even offered to share it with me if I'd give him another go. I ran to the bathroom and cleaned...I had to clean myself up. My clothes were in there so I dressed and left. I never said anything to anyone."

"Mother fuck. He raped you. I'm going to find that bastard and I'm going to—" Damon rose as though he was leaving now to find him. Charlie held her son close to her. No one had ever come to her rescue before and she liked the feeling.

"No! It doesn't matter anymore. I have Connor. Because of that night, I got Connor and as far as I'm concerned, that's all that happened. He gave me a gift and I can't be happier with the results."

"Does he know about your son, Charlie? I know that you are required to let him know about the baby here, but did he know that that night resulted in a child?"

She nodded to Devin. "Yes. He found out shortly after my mother...I'd been sick, you see. I thought I had the flu and it didn't seem to stop. I went to the doctor with my mother. She was pissed when she found out. She demanded that I have an abortion, then she threatened…she threatened me. Once she found out who the boy was, she took me there and demanded that he marry me. Needless to say, that didn't happen."

"She told my momma that if she didn't tell her then she was gonna make her have an accident. She said that I was a sin and that I didn't need to be a…a rememberer of her being a slut. You have to tell them everything, Momma. I hate my grandma and she knows it."

Charlie smiled. Yes, her mother did indeed know Connor hated her. She smiled at the memory of that phone call when she'd tried in vain to get her to give him up. She'd gotten more than she bargained for when Connor had answered.

"You told her off, did you, son? Good for you. When you and your mother marry Damon, I'll be your grandma. I think you should start calling me that right now. Come over here and sit with me. I think your momma needs to pace, don't you, dear?" Margaret said.

"That mean old woman told me that if I hadn't been born, then she would have had her little girl back. I told her that she could have had me too, but I didn't think she should have me and momma anymore. Told the old bat to go get…Momma?"

"Oh don't stop now. You've gone this far. What did you tell your grandma?" Charlie was going to have to talk to Jamie. Connor didn't need encouragement when it came to speaking his mind.

"I told her to get away from us and to leave us alone. She was gonna smack me, but Momma grabbed her hand. I don't think I've ever seen my momma move that quick before. Well, 'cept the time I was about to get hit by that bastard. She moved quick like then too."

"Connor. Jamie, please don't help him." He grinned at her and then winked. "Anyway, after that, she kicked me out. I lived with Jorden and her family long enough to finish high school, then I packed up Connor and we moved to another city. We lived in a little apartment with some help from the government, and I worked and went to school. It took us a long time, but I graduated from nursing school and had a good job at a large hospital working in the ER department. Connor was three and in preschool during the day and at Jorden's house at night when I had to work midnights. We were just getting it together when Anthony Ormond came into the picture."

"You're an RN? That's wonderful, isn't it, Damon? And you did it in three years? I'm impressed. It must have been difficult raising a kid on your own and going to school full time."

Charlie looked at Spencer oddly. He'd said that as if he knew something she didn't. She looked over at Damon and he was glaring at his brother. She started to ask, but Pi came into the room.

"Missy Dane, I have food. I don't know why you people eat out when you come here to eat again. You waste money on that. If you want to spend money, you give to me. Missy Dane say I can open restaurant when I have half money."

"I told you that I would foot the bill if you wanted to open a restaurant. You're the one who said half. I swear, Pi, you get more irritating every day. If I didn't love you so much, I'd send you back to China in a heartbeat."

"Who watch baby for you? Beside, Mister Jamie love me. He tell me that he not run house so big without me. He not let you send me back."

Charlie burst out laughing. She knew without a doubt these two went at it like this often. She could also tell the two women were close, and that they loved each other a great deal. When she stood to go into the dining room with the others, Damon held her back. She was suddenly very nervous.

He stood very close to her after everyone left the room. She wanted to touch him, but held back. He looked down at her as he held her hand and twisted her new ring around on her finger.

"Are you all right? If you want, we can wait until later to…I wish we were alone. I'd very much like to see you naked right now. It's everything I can do not to throw you over my shoulder and take you to the closest wall, room, hell, even this floor looks good right now."

She burst out laughing again. She didn't expect that, him to want her after what she had told him. Charlie reached up, wrapped her arms around his shoulders, and stepped closer to him.

"I feel the same way. Do you think anyone would miss us if we locked the door and had sex right here on the floor? I need you very badly."

His growl sent a shiver down her spine. When he pulled her body tight against his, she could feel his erection hard against her belly. She felt her body respond to his; her nipples tightened and her breasts swelled. And the dampness of her panties told her she was wet and ready for him anywhere she could get him.

Damon kissed her then. His mouth opened over hers and his tongue moved in and out like she wanted his cock to do to her pussy. She rocked against him and felt his hands tighten on her hips then move down to her ass and lift her. Wrapping her legs around his hips was as natural to her as breathing.

"Christ, woman! The things you do to me. I'm going to go down on you, but you have to be quiet when you come. Take off your pants and sit in that chair."

The urgency in his voice made her hurry. When the zipper gave her a little issue; she had to laugh at him. She thought she could come with him just growling at her. When her pants were down, she didn't even make it over to the chair before he dropped in front of her. His hiss made her remember what she'd had done today.

"I thought we were getting a haircut when I agreed to this. Then I couldn't think past you seeing me like this. I know it's weird, but I...oh, Damon, please."

His finger pushing into her made her tremble. And when he kissed the bare area just above her slit, she thought she was would fall over. He still hadn't said anything when he inserted another finger into her.

"If I'd have known about this earlier, I...you have no idea how much I want to taste you like this. I want to open your soft lips and suckle at your clit until you scream my name. Then I want to fuck you, hard and fast until neither of us can move. Charlie, you're soaking my hand, your juices are running down my arm. I want to savor this gift. I want to take my time eating you. So for right now, I want you to come. I want you to come around my fingers and know that as soon as I can manage it, I'm going to slam my cock deep inside of you until you come so many times you pass out from it. Come, baby, come now."

She grabbed his head and held on. Her release slammed through her so hard it was everything she could do not to scream. Ramming her fist into her mouth, she bit hard so she wouldn't make any noise. When Damon leaned forward and licked her clit, she came again. This time, she did collapse. Had he not grabbed her, she wasn't sure what would have happened.

"Damon, if you savor me later, you may end up killing me." His laughter made her smile. When he kissed her, she could feel his hunger and it added to hers. She wondered if it would always be like this between them and knew that it would be.

~~~

Anthony got back into his car. Damned woman was going to pay for this. He slammed his bloodied hand down on the steering wheel several times before he felt marginally better. Taking several deep breaths, he closed his eyes to review what he'd just learned. He nearly hit the wheel again in frustration.

All he'd been able to get from the clerk behind the counter was that there were women running all the time and that maybe he should just give up on finding this one. Well that had been her opinion before Anthony had changed it for her at any rate. It had been too easy to get the woman to beg him to not hit her anymore. And easier still to kill her.

Anthony hated to teach stupid women lessons, but if he was the only one to do it, then so be it. He'd train them one bitch at a time if he had to. He reached into the glove box and pulled out the container of sanitary wipes. He meticulously cleaned the blood from his hand and forearm. There was blood on his service ring and that made him want to go back in and hit the dead woman again. He took pride in his control not to do so. He took all the wipes and stuffed them into his pocket. Starting the car, he drove to the local police department. He would ask his fellow officers to help.

He of course wouldn't tell them that she was his. He wouldn't want it to get around the Anthony Ormond had lost one so he told them the same story he'd told all the other departments along the stops of the bus. The only one he hadn't stopped in was Columbus. That bitch that had called him about Charlotte had told him that she was going to Washington. He wished now that he'd gotten her name. Something like that, a lie to him, shouldn't go unpunished. They were most helpful, even going so far as to pull up the cameras in that station over the past five days to see if the thief had gotten off in their fair city.

He was driving back to his hotel when he remembered something else. The boy, he'd not looked for the boy who could have been getting off the bus instead of his mother. Anthony had made sure the kid would remember his belt across his backside, but that didn't mean the lesson had taken. When he got them back, he was going to have to buy an extra leather belt to administer their punishments to them. One just would not be enough and if the boy died, then so much the better.

He hated that his Charlotte had been sullied. Of course her mother had had no problem telling him all about the boy who had ruined her. She went on and on about how she had begged Charlotte to get rid of it, but she wouldn't listen to her. Now that Charlotte had a nice young man like him wanting her, maybe it wasn't too late to give him up for adoption.

Anthony thought his idea was much simpler. Just get rid of him and then there would be no lingering thoughts about getting him back. Killing kids, especially tainted ones like her boy, didn't need to be messing with nice young girls when he was old enough to fuck one. Didn't need his kind lowering the gene pool when men like Anthony worked so hard to make the strongest survive. Yeah, the boy was just a heartbeat away from death. And for all that his Charlotte had put him through concerning the boy, then she needed to see him dead to believe that Anthony had her best interest, at heart. Of course this was after he beat him and her both.

He got back to the hotel and pulled out his notebook. The tabs along the outer edge were a little tattered, but he could still read them. At the front of the book was a list of names. All but one had been marked out. Charlotte's name was the only one there at the bottom. The other ten names were of women who had failed the test and had had to be eliminated. The next tab had the list of things they'd done to be crossed off the list.

He kept this one and used it to measure the other women that he thought might make a good suitable wife for him. Nothing but the best for the future commanding officer of the police department, so he was meticulous in keeping a record of what that women would need to be.

The next two tabs were where he'd gotten rid of the bodies and how he had done it. These lists were important because he had to make sure that he didn't use the same modus operandi, or MO, twice, and he didn't want to accidentally dig up one body when trying to dispose of another. That could be messy.

The last tab was new. He'd never had to keep a running list of things to punish a bitch for before. No one had escaped him before so he'd simply given them their punishments right then and there. The top of this list was, Running away—twenty-five lashes. He'd started out with five, but the longer she was missing, the more he'd add to it. When he found his Charlotte, she was going to have a lot of things to pay for, a lot of them.

Chapter 11

Damon knew that at least Byron knew what they'd been doing. He couldn't help but feel proud of the fact that Charlie looked like she'd just been thoroughly fucked. He knew that he did as well. Not that he minded too much. He was a little frightened by the idea of being Connor's father and being a good husband for Charlie. But he knew that he loved them and that was going to be enough.

Pi handed him a huge platter of food and then one to Charlie. She looked at the older woman with a slight dazed look and Damon burst out laughing. He'd been doing that a lot lately, just laughing.

"She makes us everything under the sun and then expects us to eat it all and give her an opinion. It's all very good. Just eat what you want and she'll be happy." Damon nodded to Charlie.

Tonight's menu consisted of chuen guen, or spring rolls, jar choi liang poon mein, or spicy cold noodles, and Black Satin Chicken, or yau gai. The Black Satin Chicken was an integral part of all Chinese dinners, almost like a focal point of the table. Where Americans might have a vase of flowers on the table, this was served in its place. Charlie loved everything.

"You were saying that Anthony came into your life at a hospital and that you were just getting it together. You mean you didn't know him before that? That all these problems are something in his own mind?" Nick asked as he blew on something for one of his children.

"He brought in this man...I can't remember his—Jim Milford, he was Jim Milford," Charlie said as if she'd suddenly remembered. "Anyway, Anthony brought him in because he claimed that he had resisted arrest and that Anthony had had to subdue him. Jim kept saying that Anthony had beaten him up after pulling him out of his car through the window that he had broken with his gun. I didn't believe or care what either man said. My job was to put his arm back together.

"As I was cleaning up the wound, Anthony kept talking to me. I didn't want to be rude, but I didn't like him. It had nothing to do with what he was saying. It was the itchy feeling he gave me when he got too close. I had to ask him several times to step away from me. Later that night, I guess after his shift, he came back. He offered to take me home and I refused him. He kept showing up, even on my days off. Then one day, he came by with Connor."

"He took your son? How on earth did he manage that? And I'd sue that daycare center for even letting him go with a stranger." Devin had jumped up so quickly that Charlie had flinched. Damon glared at his brother and then took Charlie's hand. She smiled at him and he thought he wouldn't have to murder his brother. Not yet at any rate.

"He had a badge. He's a cop. Anthony is a state trooper and he told them that I'd been hurt at work and he was there to get Connor and bring him to my work. When he got there, I threatened him. I told him if he came near us again, I'd have to go to his boss. The next night, I got a speeding ticket. My car had been in the shop for several days by then. I didn't have the money to get it fixed yet and the owner of the shop was letting me make him payments. He'd work on it until the money ran out then I'd pay him more. When I mentioned this to the officer, he took back the ticket and changed the date to the previous week. This went on for several days. I went to the police station and was advised by the guy at the desk to just give Anthony what he wanted. It was easier that way. I should have run then. Four days later, he kidnapped Connor and told me that I was to pack my stuff and move in with him or he'd kill my son. I tried to get help from the police and they simply turned their backs on me. I moved in. When he left for work two days later, that was the first time we ran."

"How many times have you left him, Charlie? I'm assuming that this isn't the second time, is it? And how far did you get?" Cait asked before Damon could.

"Not far the first time. We got as far as the bus station. He'd only slapped me that time. Then at night, or when he went to work, he'd tie me to the wall. Connor would be close enough for me to care for, but little else. He hated Connor right from the beginning. The second time we got on the bus and I paid dearly for that one. The third and fourth times, we nearly made it across the state. The beatings got progressively worse with each failure until he started threatening to hurt Connor. When I figured that out, we got away for ten days."

107

"That's when I met Anthony," Dane interrupted here. "He was the man I told you all about that Markus had kidnapped me for. Markus was terrified of Anthony and he wanted me to find this woman. When Cait brought me the clothing to read, I felt the same signature on them that had been from where he had touched me in the basement. I didn't help him then and wouldn't have either, but I can track him now. He's insane to say the least and...well, Charlie isn't the first woman he's done this too. I don't know what happened to them, but I have the feeling that they didn't 'measure up' and he killed them. He feels that he is doing the world a favor by ridding it of the weaker sex. By eliminating them, he is going to breed a stronger male population that will be just like him."

Dane moved to sit on James' lap as she spoke. When Jamie started rubbing her belly, Damon watched Dane relax. It was a birthing technique and he was glad to see that his baby brother was paying attention in class. Then he realized what was being said.

"Wait! You all knew about this? You all knew that this man was coming here and you never told any of us?" He started to move toward Charlie and Connor was suddenly there.

"You stay back. You stay away from my momma or I'll hurt you. I won't let you hurt her."

Damon took a step back. "I wouldn't hurt your mother, Connor. This is between her and me. Please let the adults talk about this. You need to—"

He was suddenly on the floor, the coffee table lying on his lap. He didn't move. He had seen Connor drop his shoulder and charge him, but he didn't think Connor would be able to budge him. He'd underestimated the kid in both his strength and his anger.

"Connor Joshua Kirkpatrick! You will tell him you're sorry right now. We do not use violence to get what we want. You'll—"

"It's all right Charlie. This is between him and me. Connor, I'd like a word with you, please. In private."

His brother Jamie helped him up. None of them said anything, though Damon noticed that Nicky was pissed. He wasn't sure if it was directed at him or Connor, but he would stay out of it. Damon looked down at Connor who stood looking for all the world like he was going to the chair. Damon pointed to where Jamie had told him the study was. Connor led the way. When Charlie started to follow, Damon stopped her.

"We'll be fine. This is between us. He'll be fine with me." He hoped.

Damon had never had to deal with a child on his own before. Unless they were hurt or sick. This was an angry child, someone who trusted little and didn't have a father of his own. When the door closed behind them, he told Connor to take a seat.

He came around the front of the desk and leaned against it. He looked down at the little boy. And tried to think how to best handle this. Damon stood up and took off his belt. He watched Connor pale, but he didn't move from his seat. He handed him the belt.

"Connor, do you know what this is used for? What I use this for? I know you understand that it's a belt, but what do I use it for?"

"You can hit me with it, but it won't keep me from protecting my momma. I'm not going to let anyone hurt her again. You ain't no different than he was."

"I don't want anyone to hurt her either. I'm in love with your momma, Connor. I won't hurt her. Ever. She means too much to me to hurt her. But back to the belt. I want you to know that all I will ever use it for is to keep up my pants. I will never hit anyone with it. I will especially never hit you or your mom with it."

"He hit her. He told her that he loved her too. Then he hit her. He used the belt on her all the time and then his fists. I'm not going to let her hurt like that again."

"Neither will I. I want you to trust me, Connor. If it makes you feel better, I'll get rid of my belts, whatever it takes to make you know that I won't hurt her. I want to protect her as much as you do."

Connor squirmed in the chair and looked everywhere but at Damon. He let him. Damon was doing some squirming of his own. He sat down in the chair next to him.

"You gonna punish me? I didn't mean to hurt you. I just can't stand it when…she's all I got. I should have…I wish I could have helped her before. But I let her down. I should have…I should have…"

Damon reached over, picked Connor up, and pulled him into his lap. He was stiff at first, but after a few seconds, Connor turned and put his arms around Damon's neck and started to cry. His heart ached for the boy. He held him while he cried his heart out and then held him when he was finished.

"I'm sorry, Damon. You must think I'm a big baby. Mr. O, he used to hurt me when I cried. Please don't tell my momma."

"Never. Men cry too. I have on occasion, but that's between you and me. One time, my brother Byron knocked me in the head with a book. I didn't cry in front of him, but I could have."

They sat like that for a few minutes. Then when Damon's cell phone went off, signaling that he had a text message, he pulled it out and read it. He burst out laughing and showed it to Connor.

"Charlie is going to storm in there if you don't tell me things are fine." It was from Byron.

"We'd better go back, huh? She's going to be mad at me when I go back out. Maybe you should just tell me what my punishment is too. Hers has to come first though. She's my momma."

"I'm not going to punish you. You were protecting the woman you and I love. I can't fault you for that. And let me talk to your mom. Maybe we can work out a deal on this one. But Connor, she's right, we don't settle things with violence. Words work better. Well, most of the time. Sometimes my brothers and I fight. But we usually end up having more fun than anything. And I have to patch them up. I have been known to lessen their pain meds just to be mean. Now that is between the two of us." They were laughing when they walked out the door.

Connor ran to his mother and hugged her. Damon didn't know what Connor told her, but she seemed satisfied with it. Damon sat back down in the big, winged chair and as Charlie walked past him, he pulled her into his lap and held her there. He thought she needed a hug, but he was sure he needed one worse.

"All right. So fill us in on what we need to know. And from now on, I think when we have discussions about this bastard, they should be in a group setting. We can all be kept up to date and there are no surprises for those of us a little late coming into the picture." Damon kissed Charlie's hand and winked at Connor. He had a family and so long as there was breath in his body, he was going to keep them all safe. First thing Monday, he was having a better security system put into the house. Also, he needed to hire someone to keep an eye on Charlie and Connor.

At around two in the morning, they all were shown to their rooms. Dane told Charlie that if she wanted to sleep with Damon, she'd have to sneak to his room after Margaret was asleep. Dane had put the older woman on the other hall to give Charlie the extra help. She'd never been any good at sneaking and she was happy for the help.

Charlie was still trying to work up the nerve to go to his room when he opened her door and slipped inside. She was shocked and excited. He looked at her with such hunger, she thought she would melt if he didn't touch her soon. But there was no way she was going to make it easy for him.

"What are you doing in here? Your mother is just down the hall. What would you have done if she had seen you? She was very explicit on you not coming to my room."

Instead of answering her, he kissed her. His tongue swept in her mouth and rolled along hers. As he backed them to the bed, he started to untie the belt at her waist and then take her robe off. Her body was on fire for his and he hadn't even touched her yet.

"I've thought about your naked pussy all evening. You aren't going to deny me having a taste of it, are you? I want to bury my mouth over your mound and fuck you with my tongue. I want to slide my fingers up into your hot pussy and feel your juices coat my hand. Then I want to drink from you, close my mouth over your clit, and have your juices fill me. You wouldn't want to deny me all that, would you?"

Her pussy wept more, so much more that her thighs now had it trickling down them she was so wet. Sliding her hand between the two of them, she cupped his cock and squeezed him. He rocked into her hand. Over and over he rocked as he stripped her out of the gown she had on as well. When she stood before him naked and bare, he stepped back and looked at her.

"You're beautiful. Lie on the bed for me, raise your arms above your head, and open your legs. I want to feast on you, Charlie. I want to have my fill of you before I fuck you."

Her heart was pounding and she could barely catch her breath. When she lay the way he wanted her to, she watched as he climbed on the bed and settled between her open thighs. He pulled his shirt up and over his head and her mouth watered at the sight. She had to grip her fingers together to keep from reaching for him.

"Damon, please do something. I'm dying here with need. I want to feel your cock inside of me in the worst way. Please stop teasing me."

He slid his finger into her and she rocked up to meet him when he moved in and out of her. She felt a second then a third finger slide in and he moved down to settle between her legs. When Charlie felt him pull her nether lips open, she heard him moan.

"You're so wet, baby. I can see your juices flowing with your new look. Would you keep your pussy bare like this for me? I want to go with you the next time you have this done."

Her body responded to his words and she felt her climax moving over her. She wanted it, wanted it so badly that she whimpered when he removed his fingers. But when his tongue speared into her, she came up off the bed. Her climax ripped through her so quickly that she had to pull the pillow over her mouth to keep from screaming. He never stopped what he was doing and even slid his fingers back into her. Still riding on the first one, the second, then a third climax took her to limits she'd never been before. When Damon pulled away and got up off the bed, she looked up at him. His pants came off in seconds and when he opened the condom, she reached for the packet and started to open it.

"Baby, I'm so close that if you play too much, I'm going to come all over you and not inside of you where I really want to be. I swear when we get home, I'll make it up to you. But I want you to roll over and put your ass up for me. I'm going to fuck you hard and fast."

After sheathing him in a condom and with a quick kiss to the tip, she rolled to her belly and then up on her knees. She put her head down on the mattress and watched him. He pushed her legs apart and then grabbed her hips. In one quick move, he was hard inside of her. Charlie felt him touch her deeper than he'd ever been. When he started to rock gently at first, her body needed more. Pressing back against him with every surge forward, it wasn't long before he was moving in her fast and frantic. When he leaned across her back, reached between her legs, and pulled on her clit, she came apart. As she was coming down, he bit her on the shoulder and brought her with him this time. Collapsing on the bed with his heavy weight on top of her, she had never been happier. Her body lax and sated, she fell into a deep, dreamless sleep.

Chapter 12

Anthony wasn't getting anywhere. He'd had to go home and fix it with his boss about taking some time off. He'd had to admit that he was having family issues and that his wife had left him, taking his son. He didn't want them to know his business, but it seemed to open a few doors with the others to know that he had a family. If he didn't find Charlotte soon, he wouldn't have one. The drive back across the country was making him exhausted. He pulled into Illinois on Thursday afternoon. It had taken him driving around the city for two hours trying to find something to eat to realize it was Thanksgiving Day and everything was closed down. He had to settle for a pizza and beer.

The beer hadn't been bad, but the pizza was shit. He'd been half tempted to go to the pizza place and beat the shit out of the person who'd made his dinner. He knew that it wouldn't do him any good so he stayed put. He had a long drive tomorrow and he didn't have time to teach some moron a lesson. At least not this trip. Besides, he wanted to get an early start in the morning to get to Columbus by dinner.

~~~

Charlie came down to the kitchen the next morning and found Dane drinking a glass of iced tea. Her flushed face and sweaty forehead had Charlie come to her immediately and check her head. Dane just laughed.

"I'm fine. Jamie just went to get something from the car. He...he and I...never mind. Jamie is very happy this morning. I'm sure about as happy as Damon was this morning when I saw him sneaking back to his room."

Charlie blushed. She hadn't even heard Damon leave this morning. He was gone when she got up and his pillow was cold, that's all she knew. She pulled a glass from the cabinet and poured her own tea. Then she sat down next to Dane.

"What are your plans now that you and Damon are going to get married? I mean, are you going to work? You wouldn't have to, by the way. The Grants are very wealthy. I'm not being nosey, just wondering for myself."

"I hadn't thought of it. I don't...I guess if I did decide to go to work, it would be at the hospital somewhere. I know that I could get hired on. My grades were good. I'd just have to take my boards for Ohio. I hadn't thought of it really, but I would work. Connor is my responsibly and I'd have to make sure he's cared for."

Charlie knew that Damon liked Connor, but he was her little boy. She needed to get him enrolled in school and then get him some clothes. Everyone had been very generous, but she needed to get on her own two feet. She was lost in thought when she heard the back door open and Jamie walked in.

"Hey, Charlie. Mom has decided that Thanksgiving is going to be held here this year and I was hoping that I could get everyone to pitch in and help Pi. Love the woman to death, but I think we all want traditional stuff. Dane is good at organizing, but I don't want her doing it all by herself."

"I'd love to help. I can cook very well. If you have everything, I can get a start on the bird and then when the others get up, we can work from there. This is a wonderful kitchen to work in."

"Wonderful. But first, I want you to come with me. I have something I need to show you. Jamie, go get your brothers up and then you guys go to your mom's and get the stuff. And make sure you make Mrs. Poole comes back with you. Tell her that I need her to make the gravy."

After they bundled up in winter coats, the two women walked over to the pool house. There was construction stuff still around, a concrete mixer, and a large dumpster. And there were still a lot of empty pallets and something that looked like a big heater, covered now that it was no longer being used. Dane unlocked the door for them and stepped back to let Charlie enter.

The room was white. There was no other way to describe it, white furniture, white carpet, and white walls. Charlie put her hands behind her back and walked around the room, careful not to touch anything. The white shelf surprised her; there were white framed black and white pictures of the Grants and of other events. She was even more surprised to find one of Connor with Spencer and Cait's little girl, Meggie. She nodded to it then looked back at Dane.

"I took it the other day when he was at their house. Meggie loves him. She said that he is coming along nicely

119

with his sign language lessons. He's a wonderful little boy. Charlie, do you know what this room is?"

"It's your white room, your room to relax and to refocus. I've read about these in college, of course. I would imagine that you would need a room like this more than most would. And your view, it's perfect."

"You've not touched anything. Not even to pick up any of the pictures to look at them. Why not? Most people would have."

Charlie thought about it before she answered. She'd heard what Dane could do. Dane had even told her about her ability when they had all gotten together at the house last week. She wasn't sure if she believed it or not, but Dane obviously did. But the question, why hadn't she touched anything?

"I'm not saying that I believe you, but I would assume that you had this room as a sterile environment. And I thought that my emotions or touches would somehow negate that for you. You need to come here and get away. If I brought myself in here, then you'd have me in here with you. Right?"

"Yes. That's correct. My grandmother had one, a room like this. Hers was in the house. It's a room of tapestries that she and my grandfather collected over the years. I don't know that over the years with Jamie and our child I won't add to it, but for now, this works for me. I want to hire you to work for me, Charlie. I need someone for my practice."

Charlie stopped and turned to look at her. Dane had sat down on the white love seat and was rubbing her belly.

Charlie remembered that. Rubbing Connor when she was pregnant made her feel so centered and relaxed.

"I wasn't aware that a psychologist needed a nurse. I thought you guys just sort of made your own assessments and all. And I'm not so sure that I'd make a good receptionist either."

"No, that's not what I need you for. I want you to be there for me. I want to take on more cases that involve missing children and sometimes it's unsafe for me. I sort of go into a trance and when I do, I forget how to come back home. I'd like to hire you to be there in the event that would happen."

"You want me to babysit you while you go into a trance. I take it this has happened before. How bad did it get and how did you get back, as you call it?"

"Jamie and his brothers broke down the door to my room and then Jamie put me in a cold shower. I had gone far that time. And when I was kidnapped and beaten, I nearly died. I need someone who cares for me to watch over me. Pi makes me too crazy and I'd never get her out of this room to concentrate, but you, I think you would be perfect."

Charlie sat down on the couch when Dane patted the place beside her. She didn't know what to say. No one had ever thought she was perfect for anything. Well, Connor did most days, but she was sure that would change when he got to be a teenager, but for now, she was perfect.

"Charlie, I can tell what you're thinking. Not because I can read your mind, but because of the emotions running across your face. I do think you'll be perfect. If you want to discuss it with Damon, that's okay too. I won't be opening my practice until I can find someone and I hope it's you."

"I need a job. I need to provide for my son. I can't expect Damon to keep him. He's not his son. I'd like the job. But I have to tell you that Connor comes first. If he's ill or needs me, then I can't leave him. Is that okay?"

"Of course. I wouldn't expect anything different. And Charlie, I think you're underestimating the relationship between Connor and Damon. I think Damon already plans to provide for Connor. He really likes the kid. We all do."

Charlie knew he was liked by them. He was a great little boy, but she didn't expect anyone to help her with him. He was her responsibility, not anyone else's.

Charlie worked with the others in the kitchen most of the day. They laughed and joked, talked about the new babies, and told stories about each other. She never felt out of place or not a part of the family. And when they sat down to dinner, everyone talked over each other, helped with the others' children, and even cleaned up together. Several times she went to check on Connor only to not be able to pick him out of the crowd of children playing in the gaming room. She'd never had a family of her own, nothing like this, and she realized she was happy to be a part of this one.

Chapter 13

The crowds of people were making him nuts. Limos and drivers and overdressed and overdone people walking in front of cars like they friggin' owned the place. Anthony had heard there was a thing going on at the Polaris Center, some stupid charity thing to help abused women.

Anthony snorted. Abused women, that was an oxymoron if he'd ever heard one. A woman who complained she was being abused wasn't being disciplined enough as far as he was concerned. If they'd just learn their place, a man wouldn't have to hit them so much.

He was maneuvering between streets to get to his hotel when he saw a woman with a kid. He noticed her because she was so beautiful, but then someone honked their horn at him and he lost her in the crowd. Now that was a woman he'd like to have in his house. He'd bet she'd be able to keep house and him satisfied in his bed.

Anthony was unlocking his door, still thinking about the woman a short time later. He turned on the television and there was a big deal going on about the event. He started to turn it to some of the pay per view stations when the woman came into the camera view again. Damn, she really was beautiful. Blond hair cut short, form-fitting black dress with legs that went on for miles. While he didn't approve of showing so much skin and women should never cut their hair, he thought they both suited her. When the camera focused on the kid again, Anthony nearly fell off the bed. It was the kid.

Mother fuck. Her fucking brat was on television. He picked up the remote and hit rewind, seeing if he could catch his Charlotte somewhere. When the camera flipped back to the woman and paused, he looked at her. It was her, his Charlotte.

He looked at her now, really looked. The smile on her face irritated him for some reason. He also didn't like the way the man standing next to her was touching his woman. Anthony moved closer to the set and tried to will the woman to look directly in the camera so that he could see her face. When she finally did, his breath caught. He never would have thought she was that beautiful, that glamorous.

He kept watching the program. He would catch glimpses of her now and then. Always with the same group of people, the same man. He watched the brat walking around between the adults and wondered who they were to her and the boy.

When the man leaned down and kissed his Charlotte, he lost it. His temper had always been right on the edge concerning her and to see that she had replaced him so quickly made him lose control. Taking the remote, he threw it at the television. The screen shattered and the lights popped off and on. It wasn't enough. He picked up the chair and threw it through the window. As soon as the glass shattered, he knew he'd made a mistake.

He was sitting on the bed when the knock came at the door. He was hoping it was the fat fuck that had checked him in and was happy that it was. Inviting him into the room, he shut and locked the door. Couldn't be a more perfect way to work off some anger than to take it out on an asshole.

"There a problem here? Seems like there was a lot of noise coming from this room. Wanna tell me what happened to the TV and the window? Looks like there was a fight or something."

"No, not a fight. Not then at any rate. I was watching the set when something I saw made me a little pissed off. Your timing couldn't be more perfect," Anthony said as he pulled his belt out of his pants loops.

"My timing? How do you figure—"

The first slap of the belt caught the fat fuck across the face. His cheek opened immediately and blood spilled out. The second he hit the floor, Anthony drew back the belt and hit him four more times—his face, arms, and fat gut again and again. The buckle was huge and it made perfect marks on any fatty place it touched. When the young man rolled to his back, Anthony actually laughed out loud. Each time Anthony's arm went up and then down, the young man moaned until he didn't make any more noise. Anthony continued, on and on until he couldn't raise his arm anymore.

Staggering over to the bed, Anthony dropped down onto it and then fell back against the mattress. He laid there with a smile on his face, his cock harder than it had ever been. Opening his pants, he pulled out his aching cock and began to jerk hard on it, the way made smoother, slicker with the blood on his hand. When his climax hit him, his cum shot into the air and dropped back down onto his body, hot and thick. When he was sated, he closed his eyes and fell into a deep sleep.

Two hours later, rested and relaxed, Anthony stretched out and sat up on his bed. Looking down at the man now dead on the floor, he smiled again at the memory. When he stood up and stripped off his clothes, he stepped over to the body and kissed Tim on the forehead before heading to the shower. After he was cleaned up with fresh clothes on, he looked at the mess Tim had made.

Calling the front desk, he had them call the glass company and put a new window in. He told them that he and Tim had come to an agreement and he was going to fix the window and nothing else would be said. "Bad day," he'd explained, and left it at that.

It took him three hours to get the room cleaned back up, leaving the body of the clerk in the bathtub to be found later. Dressed once again in his blond wig and ball cap, Anthony used one of the credit cards he'd kept from one of his failures. It was the least they could do after all the work he'd put into them only to be disappointed again. Allison James paid for it all. *Thank you very much, Ally dear.* Anthony was nearly to his next stop when the body was discovered and all hell broke loose.

Anthony needed to find out who the people his Charlotte was with. But most importantly who she had let kiss her when she was engaged to him. Her list was getting longer by the day and when he found her...well, it seemed his poor Charlotte had gone too far. She, like the others, had cheated on him once too often. Pulling into the little hotel along the highway, he got a room as far away from the front desk as possible. This time, his room was being paid for compliments of his Charlotte.

He'd been making the minimum payment on her cards since she'd moved in with him. He never knew when he would need to make a purchase on something nice and since he was making the payment, he felt it was his right to use the card as he saw fit. He knew that she thought the cards were cancelled. That's what made it so perfect. And he was doing her a favor. Her credit rating was good and they had increased her credit line to three times what she'd had before him. Having his mail delivered to a post office box kept her from knowing that he had several other credit cards with different names on all of them. Most of the cards were women he'd asked to marry him and they had failed him in some way. Others were just cards he'd come across in his line of business.

By eight o'clock on Friday night, Anthony was sitting in a nice hotel room having just eaten a huge steak at a local restaurant called Muddy Misers. Anthony had porn on the television and he had jerked off three times just thinking about the fat fuck he'd killed across town. Yep, life was good.

~~~

"Have I told you how lovely you look? You do, you know. Sexy too. I would love to find a place to take you so that I can personally show you how sexy you look."

They were dancing, he and Charlie. He'd been pleasantly surprised to know that even Connor could slow dance. He'd asked Meggie to dance when Damon and Charlie had gotten up. Connor looked handsome in his tux and seemed to really enjoy wearing it. His mother had fussed at him several times about getting dirty before Damon pointed out that he'd bought the tux and dry cleaning was fairly cheap.

Damon loved having Charlie in his arms whether she was naked or clothed, though he preferred naked. He pulled her closer to him so that she could tell how much he thought of her being sexy. Her flush at feeling his erection made him smile again. Damn but she was beautiful when she pinked up like that.

"Will you behave? I swear, you're worse than Connor with a new toy. We just had sex before we left your house. Three times, I might add. I had to redo my hair twice and I swear that every one of your brothers knew why we were late getting here."

"I'm sure they do. Though I guess they must have their timing better than me. I'll have to work on it. You do know that each one of them had sex before they got here too? I'll have to work on my timing, that's all. And as for you being my toy…I think I like the sound of that. I could get you all wound up then play with you for hours. Oh yeah, I like that idea. When can I play with you again, Charlie?"

She was doing that flustered thing again. He thought that was perhaps the cutest thing she did when she was upset. Her face got pink and she chewed on her lower lip while she glared. Then she would try and say something that usually turned out to be gibberish.

He had laughed at her when she'd done it a couple of days ago. He certainly wouldn't do that again anytime soon. At least not where she could hear him at any rate. Then there was the thing she did when he knew he'd screwed up. He'd seen his mother do it once or twice when they'd been kids, but seeing Charlie do it just made him hard. Her hands went to her hips and she'd tap tap tap her foot. He didn't know if it was watching her breasts bounce in time to the tapping or the way she glared at him. Either way, he wanted to piss her off just to see her do it.

Connor had pointed out a couple more things she did when she was upset. He promised himself that he'd aggravate her tomorrow to see if he could get her to do the one where she didn't say anything but kept tsking and throwing her hands in the air. Connor had told him that when she got to that point, he'd better be careful; she was on the war path. Yes, living with these two was going to be a lot of fun.

"I wanted to tell you about a job offer I have. I'm going to take it. Dane has asked me to come work for her as her spotter. I know that's not what it's called really, but when she goes into a trance, she wants me there to keep an eye on her. I haven't told her yes yet, but I think I'm going to take it."

Damon had thought Charlie would come work for him, but as soon as he'd thought it, he realized what a bad idea that would be. They could barely keep their hands off each other around the house. He'd never see a patient if she was there with him all day. Christ, but that sounded really good one minute and really bad the next. He looked down at her when he realized she was waiting for something. He tried to remember what, if anything, she'd asked him.

"I've seen her in those trances and they can be very scary. I'm glad she's asked you to help her out. I was hoping that I could depend on you sometimes too. Come in and sub for one of the nurses when they need time off. We should also talk about getting Connor into school. I mentioned it to him the other day and I think he growled at me. He said you've been home schooling him for about two years."

"Yes. Anthony wouldn't let him go to school very much. I think he was afraid he'd say the wrong thing to the right people. Then after a while, it was just easier to teach him at home. He's really smart, but I don't know what I can afford school-wise around here. Do you know anything about the schools around your house?"

She'd been referring to the house as his house for two days. He wanted her to think of it as their house and was just about to point out to her that she could afford to send Connor anywhere she wanted when Cait walked up to them.

"I have to go. There's been an incident over at the hotel on Fifth Avenue. Will you please give Spencer a ride home? I have to take the car."

"Of course. What happened, do you know yet? I mean, I know things like this happen, but that's a really nice hotel." Damon was leading Charlie and Cait back to the table as he spoke to her.

"Not much. The owner's son was beaten to death and left in the room. There had been a disturbance and he'd gone up to check on it. They figure he's been dead less than three hours. I'll call you if I need anything."

Cait kissed them all on the cheeks and was out the door. They had to stay. The auction was the biggest fund raiser and event of the evening. The mood around the table had dropped, but each of them knew that if anyone would solve the murder, Cait would.

Three hours later and very near the end of the event, Cait called and spoke to Dane and then to Jamie. It seemed they wanted to bring Dane in to see if she could get anything from the room. Jamie didn't want his very pregnant wife to go and asked if Damon would please go with them.

"Cait said for me to take Charlie and Connor home with me," Jamie said after he handed the phone back to his wife. "She said that she didn't want her to be alone."

Damon looked over at Charlie who was talking to his mother. "Something's happened at the crime scene, or is it the crime scene? Tell me, Jamie, what's going on." Terror like he'd never felt moved through him and he suddenly wanted to grab up Charlie and Connor and run to the nearest cave and hide them.

"I honestly don't know. If I did, you know I'd tell you. Go with Dane. I know she'll be fine, but Cait said to have you come with her. Damon, I really like Charlie and Connor. I'll take good care of them."

"I know you will, Jamie. But…but I'm in love with her. I can't stand the fact that there's someone out there who wants to hurt them. We have to get this guy. We have to get him so that we can get on with our lives."

Damon drove them over to the crime scene. It was only five blocks from where they had all been tonight. He wasn't a hundred percent sure that this had anything to do with Charlie, but deep in his gut, he knew that it did. He reached over, took Dane's hand and squeezed it.

"You'll have a child. You and Charlie will have a child. I don't get premonitions often, but when I do, they're always true. I don't know what happens between now and then, but from experience, I can tell you that it'll make you stronger. If this is…if this man is a part of this crime, Damon, I'll know it."

"I know you will, kiddo. But I can't help but be terrified that he is. I've waited my whole life for Charlie and I don't want to see her hurt anymore."

Chapter 14

Charlie looked out the window of the big SUV and tried to get her emotions together. No matter what they tried to hide from her, she knew that it was Anthony. He'd found them and he'd hurt someone else because she had left him. She looked down at the ring on her finger. When Jamie spoke, she jumped slightly.

"Whatever you're thinking, stop it. You're safe and so is Connor. Damon loves you and you love him. End of story. Now, tell me how you liked the charity thing. Mom will ask me ten times what you had to say about it."

She continued to look out the window and knew what she had to do. Keeping her son safe was paramount. But she also knew that now that Damon was with her, he'd be in danger too. She wanted to have what they all had, but this man, Anthony, would hurt them if she did.

"It was lovely. I can't believe how much...Jamie, what happens if he finds me? You know as well as I do that he will eventually. And when he does, whoever is with me will be hurt too."

"How much what, Charlie? You can't believe how much what? And no one is getting to you without coming through all of us. Focus on the good, not the bad. Tell me what you liked about the function. And by the way, you might as well get used to these sorts of things. Mom wants to start having more of them in the future. Also, and don't tell her I warned you, but Dane is going to ask you to help her with the annual Mother's Day thing she's putting together to surprise Mom."

They talked about mundane things. Things in the future when she became Damon's wife, things that he thought she'd find funny. He told her stories about the men as children and the things they'd done to one another. How Damon would always be the voice of reason and would have to patch them up in the end. All the time they were talking, Charlie had half her mind on the fact that she needed to leave and how she was going to leave the only man she would ever love.

When they got to Jamie's house, he carried a sleeping Connor up to the room he'd stayed in before. Jamie had told Connor before they'd left for the event that he could have the room permanently and that whenever he wanted, he could come and stay with Dane and him. Charlie was taking off his tuxedo pants when he woke up and looked at her.

"He's found us, hasn't he? That's why Aunt Cait had to leave and Aunt Dane, right? Mr. O found us."

"You like these people very much, don't you, Connor? I'm so glad. Yes, Anthony found me. I think he might have killed someone tonight and that's why they took Dane over to the place Cait went."

She didn't know he was calling them aunt and uncle, but she was glad he liked them enough to give them that. It would make doing what she had to do much easier. She loved Connor too much to let him get hurt and Anthony had told them enough that if she ran again, he'd kill her son.

"Are we gonna run again soon? I don't wanna, Momma. I like it here a lot. Damon is really nice to me and he tells me all the time that he loves you. Can't we stay?"

She smoothed his hair from his face and marveled again at how much she loved this little person she'd made. He was all she had in the world that she was proud of and she couldn't...no, she wouldn't let anything happen to him. And doing this now hurt her more than she'd ever thought it could.

"You aren't running this time, Connor. I can't let you keep doing this. I have to—"

"No! You aren't going to leave me here. I can't be here without you, Momma. We can go now if you want, but you have to take me with you. Please, Momma, don't leave me here. I love you."

"I love you too, sweetheart. Oh Connor, you're everything to me and I don't want you...he'll kill you. Do you think I want that? Do you think I'd want to live knowing that he killed you because I ran? You have to live. You have to live for me and be happy. If he catches me this time, I won't be able to run again. He'll never let me have the opportunity to leave him. I want to know every day that you're out there somewhere being my happy little boy."

When he threw himself at her, she hugged him with everything she had. They cried in each other's arms until he fell asleep. Lifting him as gently as she could, she took him over to the rocking chair she'd seen in the corner of the room and rocked him. She told him stories of him and the things they'd done together. Then when she couldn't speak anymore, she put him to bed. Taking off the ring that Damon had given her, she laid it on the nightstand and slipped out of the room.

In the room she'd shared with Damon, she stripped out of the beautiful gown and pulled on her jeans and t-shirt. It was nearly four in the morning when she walked out of the house and down the drive. She was glad that Jamie had given her the code to unlock the door when they arrived or she was sure she would never have made it out as easily as she had. Charlie had almost a hundred dollars left of the money that they had started out with.

She wasn't naive enough to think Anthony was going to take her back without hurting her. In fact, she was reasonably sure that he would kill her when he found her. As long as Connor was all right, then she would be able to die peacefully.

~~~

Damon was just pulling up in front of the hotel when Cait came out of a room where about ten cops were milling around. She noticed Dane and him and started toward them. Someone had given her a coverall. But she was still wearing her heels. It would have been something he would have found very funny. But the blood on her front made it too real to even smile.

"I don't suppose you can pronounce. Can you? The coroner can't be here for another three hours. He's stuck at an airport in Virginia and his assistant is in the hospital.

I want to get the body to the office and get it taken care of tonight."

Damon nodded and pulled out his cell. "I just have to get it verified from someone. I've even done a few autopsies in the past. I'll ask about that as well."

He just wanted to make sure that whatever he did was legal. With his involvement with Charlie and if this man had been killed by the same man, he didn't want to screw up the case to convict.

"Hello, Damon. It's been a long time. Please tell me that you've decided to come back to work with us."

The director of OSU hospital, Justin Sawyer, had been calling weekly to see if Damon was ready to come and take over the teaching department. He hadn't been tempted at all until recently. Being home every night and on weekends sounded good now that he had a family.

"No, but I'm thinking about it. I'll come in and talk to you next week. Thomas is out of town and Peterson is sick, and the police need a quick autopsy done. I might be involved with the case due to my fiancée and her son. Would you back me if I did it for them?"

Damon wasn't worried about ethics or anything like that, but he would need to use the hospital to perform it and he didn't want to step on anyone's toes. The medical field had as many land mines as most corporations. Plus, he wanted to make sure that if he did take the job, that everyone knew right from the start he was a team player.

"Of course I will. I'll send someone to assist, that way there won't be any question as to the validity of it. Are you coming with the body or police? I need to know so that if I have to make a statement, I want to make sure they film me from my good side."

"Police. I'll let you talk to Captain Grant. She's in charge of the case. She can give you details that you can work with."

Damon handed his cell phone to Cait and walked over to Dane. She was leaning against the car and rubbing her feet. He had to smile; he'd told her not to wear those heels being eight months pregnant. When she noticed that he was smiling at her, she stood up and glared.

"I'm pregnant and it's nearly three in the morning. Of course my feet are going to hurt. If you say one more word, I'll hurt you. How much longer is this going to be?"

He laughed out loud this time. He loved the women of this family. They could be just as sweet as sugar one minute and hard as nails the next. He hugged her to him. Then he reached into his car, pulled out a pair of slippers, and handed them to her. He had bought them for himself a few days ago, but was willing to sacrifice them for her. She squealed in delight and nearly took his head off when she tossed the high-heeled shoes at him.

"Okay. Damon is going to pronounce and as soon as that happens, then we'll transport. Once that happens, Dane, you can go in. Is there anything you need before the body is taken away? I think I can get you whatever you need. According to Sawyer, Damon has been appointed acting coroner until further notice." Cait was saying this as she handed Damon back his phone.

"Wait!" Damon nearly shouted at her. "Acting coroner? How the hell did you manage that? Or do I want to know? Damn it, Cait, I said I'd help, not take over a damned department. If this comes back and bites me in the ass, I'm going to paddle yours." Her laughter followed him into the room.

The scent of blood hit him first, then the smell of bowel movement. The room reeked of them. When he stepped into the bathroom and saw the young man lying in the tub, he had to take several deep breaths before he could lean down and check for a pulse. Anyone around them could see that he was dead, but without the official pronouncement, he was presumed living.

Damon stood nearby as they pulled Tim's body out. When he was rolled over to his belly, Damon couldn't believe the damage that had been inflicted. Tim's shirt was shredded and bloodied. And through the tears, he could see where whatever had hit the young man had broken his ribs. Broken them badly enough that they stuck out like broken twigs through the skin. Large muscle tissue was torn from his back and shoulders. The back of his head was also broken and bloodied. When Damon leaned forward, he could see where brain matter had seeped from a massive contusion on the back of his head. Whoever had hit him must have been covered in blood and very strong.

"I'll ride with him. I can tell you this, it's going to be messy. First thought is blunt force trauma. Dane can come in, but I'd keep her out of the bathroom. The kid must have crapped himself. I'll get back to you as soon as I get something. And don't think I've forgotten about this thing with the coroner."

His phone was ringing as he stepped into the wagon. Frowning, he answered it, wondering what Jamie would be calling for at four in the morning. As soon as he thought it, he realized that something had happened to Charlie or Connor.

"She's gone. She fucking left after I told her we would protect her. I went to her room to check on her and the dress she had on is on the bed. I even went down to your room to see if she was there, maybe sleeping in your bed. I just checked. Connor is bundled up in the bed asleep. Damn it, Damon, I all but told her that we had her back and that she'd be stupid to run."

He rested his forehead on the top of the car and closed his eyes. He wasn't really surprised, hurt but not surprised. She'd left Connor behind and Damon knew that she would have told him she was leaving.

"Let me talk to Connor. He might know something. It's not your fault. She had it in her head to run as soon as she realized that this man was close. I can't believe she left Connor and that he let her."

It took two minutes for Jamie to come back to the phone and another couple minutes before Damon could get what he was saying. Connor was gone too. He'd put his pillows in the bed to hide that he was gone. But he left Damon a note. Jamie asked if Damon wanted him to read it.

"Yes, hurry. Stupid woman. I'm going to beat her ass for this. Taking a kid out when she knows fucking well that that man is out to get them both. What the hell was she thinking?"

"She didn't. Take him, I mean. Listen to his— 'Damon, Momma left me with you, but I can't leave her alone. That man is after her and I gotta protect her.

Momma said she loves you and so do I. I'll pay you all back like you said. Connor J. Kirkpatrick.' When you get this kid back, I'm going to give him a hug then beat his ass. Do these people have no concept of what this man could do to them if he finds them?"

Damon thought they probably had a better idea than any of them. He closed his eyes against the pain of losing the two of them. He had to find them. He had to make sure they would never feel the need to run away again.

Chapter 15

Dane walked into the room and was assaulted with the emotions of every person that had ever been in the room. Love, hurt, anger, sex, and lust—the list was endless. She closed her eyes and tried to focus on one thing at a time, trying to narrow it down to the one person she had met before. She was just getting a handle on him when she felt Cait enter the room behind her.

"Let me know what you get, Dane, and I'll write it down. The others are all out of the room. I've got them looking around the building for a weapon or whatever he might have used to kill Tim. Damon said not to go into the bathroom. He thinks the smell might be too much for you."

Dane nodded. She didn't try to have a conversation when she was searching for someone. It took too much energy and she didn't want to try to focus on too many things at once. She walked over to the blood stain on the floor and kneeled down to touch it. Cait stopped her before she did.

"That hasn't been cleared yet. I don't know what the vic had in way of diseases and if you catch something, even a cold from this, Jamie will have my hide. Make sure that if you have to touch it, you don't have any cuts on you, and that you let the EMTs clean you up after you're done."

Dane checked her fingers everywhere. She didn't think she had any cuts or open wounds on her hands, but she didn't want to take the chance either. Because she knew that once Jamie finished with Cait, he'd start on her. She smiled at the thought of Jamie when he got all protective. He was very laid back on everything except for her getting hurt. She touched the blood with her index finger.

Terror, terror like nothing she'd felt for a very long time hit her and nearly knocked her back on her ass. She had to grip the bed hard to keep upright. Once she got that feeling under control, she could sort through the other emotions.

"Tim is terrified. He's also…he's also confused and a little angry. It's a belt. Heavy, and the buckle hurts as it hits me. I can feel the hook tearing at my skin, pulling it with every one of the hits. Pain radiates from my face. I don't want to be marred. Mom. She's going to be so disappointed about the floor. The carpets have just been replaced in here. Television is broken. Window. I wonder if I can make it to the window to get away. I know I'm going to die. Death is welcome from the pain, so much pain."

Dane sat there for a minute. She knew that Cait was writing things down; the scrape of the pen across the paper was loud in the room. Dane spread her hand over the bed to stand, and felt the other man.

"Anthony laid here. Christ, Charlie! Oh God! He's going to kill her. It's all that bitch's fault that he can't get an erection when he's around her. I should have fucked her from the beginning. I can't…pain, I love the pain and the power. No one can defeat me, I'm the only one who…fat fuck, I'm not a homo, not a homo, not a homo."

Dane woke to Cait screaming at her. It took Dane a few moments to realize that Cait was saying something and then when Dane did, it still made little sense. Sitting up off the floor, she put her head in her hands and raised her hand to stop the flow of words directed at her.

"Dane, you do that to me again and I swear to Christ I will kill you. You scared the living shit out of me. I've never actually seen a woman swoon before, and I hope to all that's holy that I never do again. Your fucking eyes actually rolled to the back of your head. Are you all right?"

Dane laughed. It was all she could do. Big bad Caitlynne O'Malley Grant, big time detective and killer of scum, sounded like a little girl who had just seen her first scary movie. She couldn't wait to tell Jamie.

"Yes. Sort of. Okay, not really." Dane sat there for a few more minutes before she felt she could talk again. "Anthony is a homosexual, but he refuses to admit it. He brings women into his home hoping that one of them will give him what he feels is the right chemistry so that he'll no longer feel anything toward men. The pain and the violence aren't new to him. My mother…his mother beat him nearly every day of his young life just because she felt that at some point during the day he'd done something that warranted it and she didn't want him to think he got away with anything."

"You did that before. Before, when you were in the trance thingy. You referred to what you were feeling as if it was you. Is that normal? It took me a few seconds to realize that you weren't talking to me."

"Yes. If the emotion is really strong, it's as if I'm the person. Tim was dying and he knew it. The pain was real and it's fresh in his blood so it was easy to feel for him. That's what I can do as an empath. Anthony is insane. I don't mean that in a flippant way. He really is insane. He has emotional problems because of his upbringing, but he had a place in his mind that's dark. Almost too dark for me to want to enter. I would say that he's been killing for a very long time, probably since he was an adolescent. There were small and then larger animals in his place, the memories. He is blaming everything on Charlie and Connor right now. He's dangerous in every sense of the word."

Dane watched Cait process the information. She could almost see her filing things away, putting things in order for her mind to go over. It was like watching a computer processor and how it would retrieve the facts before moving on. Dane wondered if Cait knew she did it.

"Anthony killed Tim, that much we're sure of. He also blames Charlie and Connor for his fucked up life right now. Oh, he lost his job. He told them that he was coming out here to get his wife and son and someone pointed out that he wasn't married, never had been. We think he's done this before. Now I have to figure out a way to convey this information to the people in Illinois so that they'll know to look for others. Any suggestions?"

Dane looked around the room. Blood was everywhere, walls, bed, carpet and dresser. She figured that if he was this violent with a stranger, what would he do to someone who lived with him until he found them unworthy? There would have to be lots more blood somewhere.

"Do you know what kind of house he has? What kind of property? He'd have to have a lot of room, wouldn't he? Somewhere the neighbors wouldn't be able to hear. I can give you a couple of names that were running around in his head. There was an Alexandra and a Margo or Argo."

"Without last names, I don't think we'd have much luck...hang on." Cait opened her cell phone when it rang and Dane could tell right away that something had happened. Dane could hear a male voice, probably Damon, yelling on the other end. When she hung up, she looked pissed.

"Charlie left your house. And Connor is missing too. He left a note for Damon. It said that he loved them all very much, but he couldn't be without his momma. That she wouldn't be safe without him. Damn it. I can't keep them safe if I don't know where they are."

Dane couldn't agree more. But she could maybe find Charlie. Sometimes when someone was close to her, she couldn't read anything about them. Dane hadn't been able to read Pi for years. Moving to the door with Cait, she thought of something else.

"Anthony won't be satisfied with just Charlie. He needs Connor too. He needs to kill them both now. If he finds Connor first, he'll hold off until he has Charlie, and vice versa, I think."

"As much as I hate to say it, I hope he finds her first. If she finds him with her son, she won't be rational. I know I wouldn't. I'd tear into the bastard and get myself killed for either one of my children."

Dane rubbed her belly; the baby kicked her back. She knew that what Cait said was true. Anthony would hurt Charlie, but not enough to kill her. Even though her child was still inside of her, she knew she wouldn't be rational either.

Cait stood and helped Dane up as she spoke. "Come on. Let's go rally the troops and find our new sister. Heaven help her when Damon gets her back. I love him to death, but damn, he loves Charlie."

~~~

Charlie knew she was being followed. Whoever it was wasn't being very quiet, nor were they particularly fast. She tucked herself into a pocket of a doorway and waited for him or her. She had nearly fallen asleep when she heard someone walking close by. She was nearly on top of the person when she realized it was Connor.

"Damn it, Connor! You scared me to death. What are you doing out here? You'll get your butt back to that house and stay there until Damon comes for you. I should whip you for this. Do you have any idea what could have happened to you out at night all alone? Whose coat is this? Jamie's? You took Jamie's coat too? Oh Connor, what am I going to do with you?"

"You're out here. I don't think you're very smart right now either. Do you even have a gun or anything? How you gonna kill Mr. O if you don't have nothing to do it with? Huh? And I'm not going back. You were always telling me that we were a team. Well, you can't be a team all by yourself. I'm going with you or I'll keep running away until…until Damon puts me in prison. HA!"

Charlie doubted that Damon would put him in prison, but she knew what Connor was trying to say. He would keep running away until he got himself killed or he found her. Charlie gathered him into her arms and held him. She wasn't sure what she would do with him, but was very glad he was with her.

"All right, but we stay together. No running off and finding lovely doctors and his family to keep us patched up. I mean it, Connor. You stay with me."

"I'll stay with you, Momma, but I'm not going to promise that I won't go find somebody to patch you up if you're hurt. I'm gonna take care of you no matter what."

Charlie couldn't fault him for that. So she hugged him again and then reached out for his hand. She didn't know how she was going to hide from Anthony, and now with Connor, it would twice as hard. She knew that she would die for him; she just hoped that he wouldn't have to die for her. The thought of losing Connor was too much. They made their way to the bus station. Getting out of town had to be their first priority, but right now, all they had between them was just over a hundred dollars.

"Connor, where did you get that money? I hope you didn't take more from Anthony just in case we might need it. It's bad enough that we took what we did. I hate that we stole his money."

"No. I wouldn't take nothing from him. I got it for working for my uncles...I mean the Grants. Mr. Devin paid me for helping his wife bring in the groceries, and the others did too. I saved it for my...I just saved it."

Charlie felt bad for Connor. She knew he had been saving the money to fix up the bedroom Damon had given him. She wanted to sit down and cry for all that he had lost. She also wondered if he would ever forgive her for this.

"I'm sorry, Connor. I've been such a lousy mother to you lately. I wanted you to have so much more than me. I wanted you to...I will make this up to you. I swear I will. I just don't know...I didn't want to go live with him. I wanted us to be our own family, you and I. Why did he do this to us?"

Connor hugged her to him. He was such a great kid. She honestly didn't know what she'd do without him. Moving into the well-lit bus station, she went up to the counter and wiped at her tears. Wouldn't do either of them any good if she cried for a month, she thought. Right now she had to figure out how far they could go on what little they had on them.

"Okay, kiddo. It seems we have more choices than I thought we would. We can go to Cincinnati or we can go to Cleveland. I don't know much about either place other than one is the capitol of this state and the other used to be. What do you think, shall we flip a coin for it?"

That's how they ended up in Ohio in the first place. They'd flipped a coin to see if they went to California or they went to Washington DC. She was glad now that they hadn't gone to either. She would never have met Damon and his family if they had. And as much as it hurt to admit it, she knew she'd never love anyone again. She was glad that she had been able to see what true love was like before she died.

"Let's go to Cincinnati. I think we could run to Kentucky if we need to. We got nowhere to go up there in Cleveland but Canada and we don't have a passportal."

"Passport. But you're right. Okay, Cincinnati it is. The next bus leaves in two hours. With the tickets, we'll have about ten bucks left. Would you like to eat now or later when we get there?"

They decided to eat later. It was going to take them six hours to get to their destination and neither of them was looking forward to the long ride. They could have gotten on a quicker bus, but that was more expensive.

Chapter 16

They were all at Jamie's house an hour later except for Dane and Cait, and Damon was on his way. Dane and Cait showed up about an hour after Damon had finished up the autopsy, and he was headed toward them when Jamie called him again.

"My gun is missing, as well as my cell phone. I don't know which one of them took my coat, but my gun and phone were in the pocket. Christ, I'm so sorry, Damon."

Damon pulled over to the side of the road and tried to wrap his mind around the fact that Jamie had left a gun out where it could be taken. Damon wanted to scream at his brother, but knew that it wouldn't do him a bit of good. Damon just laid his head on the steering wheel and tried to think.

"Was it loaded? I'm assuming that it was. Jamie, do you have any idea what could happen if...I'm sorry, this isn't your fault. I just hope to Christ that Charlie got it and not Connor. Have you heard from either of them? Maybe called them?"

"Yeah, I've been trying for the past ten minutes, since I figured out the phone was missing. It goes straight to voicemail. I don't know whether or not I turned it off when I got here or if the battery is dead. And thanks, but it is my fault. I never thought…that's no excuse, but I never thought about Connor getting it. I guess I'll have to be better at this with a kid coming along. Damon, I'm so sorry. You have no idea how bad I feel."

"Call Cait. See if they can put a trace on the phone even if it's off. I'm on my way to your house right now. We have to find them, Jamie. They're everything to me."

"I know. I'm so sorry. I'll call Cait now and see what she can do. If nothing else, we can keep trying to call them and see if they'll get us."

Damon hung up and sat in his car for long moments. When he felt as if he couldn't breathe, he got out of his car and walked around the pull off. He tried to think what she would do.

First of all, she hopefully had Connor with her. He would have followed her out of the house. For some reason, Damon knew that Connor had Jamie's coat. Connor probably got downstairs and rather than run back upstairs to get his, he took Jamie's so that he could follow her sooner.

Money. He knew that Connor had some, probably about twenty bucks. When they had first come to him, Charlie had about ninety dollars on her. He wasn't sure if she had any more, but even if she did, it wouldn't be much. Where would they go with only about a hundred dollars? The first place that came to mind was the bus station. Charlie knew that way and riding the bus would be cheap. He got back into his car to go there when his phone rang again. Cait.

"I just talked to Jamie. I have a car going to the bus station now. I'm not sure if she's had time to get there or not, but someone will be there when she does. I'm going to wring Jamie's neck about the gun. Of all the stupid things to do...he needs to put in a gun safe. I'll make sure he does it as soon as we get them back, Damon. We will too."

"I was just heading to the bus station now. I don't know how far they can go. I don't think they have that much money. What did you get from the crime scene and Dane? Was she able to confirm that this guy Ormond did it?"

"Yes. He did it. I'd rather you didn't go to the station just yet. I don't want to spook her and I'm afraid if she sees you then she'll run again. Not to get away from you but to save you. She may have been right when she thought he'd hurt us to get to her and Connor. Dane says that he's been at this for a very long time. I have more information that I'd rather give you in person. He's insane, and Dane seems to think he'll kill both of them if he finds them. I have a call to his boss in Nevada. I asked him about any missing young women recently and he seemed to think that was funny. When I explained that I had a dead body out here with is boy's signature all over it and that it would look bad on his department if it got out they were uncooperative in a murder investigation, he decided to help me out. He's going to Ormond's house now to check it out. We'll find them, Damon."

"I hope so, Cait. I surely hope so. I'll come to the house, but I don't want to. I need them. I don't think...if he hurts either of them, I swear I'll...I'll...Christ, I need them back." Damon turned his car around and pulled into a parking lot. He hated to drive and talk on the phone.

"You come here and we'll talk. I have an APB out on Ormond and one on Charlie and Connor. If they're out there, we'll get them. Do you have any idea if Charlie has ever used a gun before, Damon? I'm hoping she has it, but I have a feeling Connor does. I also wonder if he even knows he has it."

Damon didn't know if either of them had any gun experience. He realized that he didn't really know that much about either of them. He was going to make it a priority when they returned. Right after he read them both the new rules he was making up in his head. First and foremost was, never, ever, ever think about running away again. He had to smile at that. He didn't think rules would go over well with either of them.

"I would think he'd know. I doubt if he'd tell his mother he has it, though. I think she'd tan his hide but good if she knew he had taken Jamie's coat without permission. No, if Connor has it, and I agree with you that he does, he is keeping it close to himself. It doesn't make me feel any better about knowing that he has it, but he isn't stupid. Not by long shot."

"No, he's not. Come to the house. We'll talk when you get here, all right?"

~~~

Connor had noticed the police there first. Charlie knew that somehow they had figured out that she and Connor would be there. Logical conclusions, she thought, since they didn't have a car and they had little money.

It got to be a game for them to see how long they could hide from the policemen, there were three of them now. First, they'd go to the shops and watch them from the windows, then they'd hide behind a magazine or whatever they could find. A couple of times, they'd nearly been caught, but Charlie had been able to lose them. She was actually terrified of what would happen if they found them, but she didn't let Connor know. Somehow, she knew that Anthony was getting closer. And the more she saw of the police looking for them, the more she knew that they had to get away.

Connor seemed nervous. More so than when they'd fled Nevada. He kept acting as if he wanted to tell her something, but would change his mind at the last minute. As much as she wanted to know what it was, it was that much more that she didn't. He would tell her in his own time, she knew. And she hoped that he would just simply tell her that he loved her, but she knew her son well enough to know that he had a secret and he was trying to figure out if she was going to be mad about it or not. She also knew that he'd tell her in his own time in his own way.

The bus was due to leave in thirty minutes. They decided to get themselves cleaned up and go to the bathroom before they left. Their first experience with riding on a milk run ride had told them that the bathrooms got really bad toward the end of the ride and if they could go now, they wouldn't have to use that one unless it was necessary.

Charlie went to the bathroom and when she came out, Connor went into the men's room to clean up and get ready. She was just getting worried when he came out. He wasn't alone. Anthony had him by the hair and a gun pointed to Connor's head. He must have hit Connor a few times. His nose was bloodied and his lip was cut. When Charlie went to lunge for her son, Anthony yanked on Connor's hair and made him whimper. She stopped where she was. Now she wanted a cop and she couldn't find any of them.

"You'll behave or I'll kill him right here. I don't want him anyway so it makes no difference to me. But you'll come along with me to save him anymore pain, won't you Charlotte, love?"

Charlie looked at the man. He looked...he looked crazed. His hair was matted and stringy, his clothes—a uniform—were wrinkled and nasty looking. She thought that he had blood on the front of it. His badge was gone and in its place was a paper one that someone, probably him, had written "Sheriff" on. His hands were also bloodied and there were a few cuts on them. He hadn't shaved in what appeared to be a week either.

"Let him go and I'll come with you. I'll not leave you again if you let Connor go. I swear it." She would give him anything he wanted for Connor to live.

"Oh you'll do that and more, my Charlotte. This is fate, you know? Fate brought us together that night and then again today. I was just going home when guess who walked back into my life? I go in to take a piss and there comes out of the stall the bane of my life, the brat. No, I don't think I'll let him go. But you're going to pay for this little trip of yours. Both of you. Now here is how this is going to work. You're going to go and buy us all a ticket to go back home and then you're going to make sure I get my job back. I don't care what you have to do to convince my boss that I need this job. I'm the best fucking person he has working for him anyway."

"All right, but I want you to let Connor go. He has nothing to do with any of this and you don't like him anyway. I'll buy the tickets for you and me. We can go anywhere you want, Anthony. It's just that I don't...I don't want you to hurt my son. He's all I have in the world."

"You got me, bitch! Me. What did I ever do to you to make you run? I provided you with three meals a day. You had a roof over your head and a warm place to sleep. I even provided for this piece of shit here and still you ran. You won't run again, you hear me? You won't run again."

Spittle ran down his chin as he spoke. She wanted to scream at him that he'd given her no reason to stay either. That in the three years that he'd made her move in with him had been a nightmare. That he'd taken everything from them, her home, her job, Connor hadn't been able to go to school. Neither of them had any friends to speak of. The one friend that she'd had was now dead because of him. The warm place to sleep had been a rag on the floor of his basement and he'd beaten them nearly every day for three long years. But she didn't. She had to think to save Connor.

"You're right. I'm sorry. I was ungrateful. But I'm coming back to you now, Anthony. I'm coming back with you and we'll make a home for ourselves—just you and me. Let Connor go and I'll do whatever you say."

"Damn right you will. But don't you think 'cause you're saying all those nice things that you won't be punished. I have a list of things you've done that you have to pay for. A very long list. And this thing here, he ain't gonna be taking up anymore of your time and my money. Oh no. That's going to be your first punishment, watching this thing die."

"You harm a hair on his head and you'll have to sleep with one eye open for the rest of your life. I will rip you apart, you cock-sucking bastard. I swear to you. Let him fucking go or I swear you'll regret making me a part of your sick, twisted life for the rest of your fucking life."

The slap was hard and quick. But she had seen it coming. Had she not moved when she did, he may have hurt her badly. As it was, all she got was a bloodied mouth. When he drew back his hand to hit her again, she kicked out at him and hit him in the knee. His scream rent the air. Several people turned to look at them, but no one came to help. When he hit her again, this time with the gun, she saw stars. Her head was spinning when she went down this time. She staggered back and felt herself flying backwards.

As Charlie tumbled across the floor and hit her head on the wall, she heard screaming. She didn't even realize it was her until later. She was having a hard time staying conscious when she noticed that there was a policeman coming up on them fast. He was shouting something, something that Charlie couldn't quite make out. That was her last thought before she saw Anthony's foot coming to her head.

Chapter 17

Connor woke to complete darkness. He wasn't afraid of the dark, but for it to be so dark, it made him very uneasy. He wasn't sure where he was, but he could feel a humming like a rumble under him. He moved around a little, but not very much. He could hear strange noises, but nothing he could recognize. Reaching around to see if he could find something to help him figure out where he was, he found the gun again. He took it out and laid it next to him.

Connor had found the gun when his momma had jumped out at him on the street. He had been terrified at first when he'd discovered it in the pocket of Jamie's coat, then he felt like he could protect his momma. He wasn't sure how to use it, but he figured he could point it and pull the trigger like they did on the television show he'd seen when he'd been staying with Damon.

Connor started to cry now. He missed Damon and wished that he and his momma could have stayed with him. He wanted more than anything to be back in that big, soft bed. He'd really liked it there and liked all the people there too. Wiping at his tears, he tried to figure out where he was. No since in crying like a little baby, wouldn't get him anywhere anyway. That's when he started to listen to the sounds around him.

First there was the sound of a horn bleeping. It sounded close at first then it seemed to fade away. That's when he noticed that he could hear music, country music like Mr. O liked. Neither Connor nor his momma liked the music, but he could recognize the noise coming from somewhere close. Listening a little harder, he could hear someone singing. It was Mr. O; he'd know that awful sound anywhere. It took Connor a few more minutes of listening to realize that he was in a car, probably in a trunk.

Connor could feel every time the car stopped then started. He'd roll to the front of the car then to the back every time it did. There was a terrible smell back here, something like the old hamburger that he'd had to take to the trash can once when his momma and he lived with Mr. O. Picking up the gun again, he cradled it to his chest and tried to think of what to do.

The policeman that had come toward them at the bus stop was dead, Connor knew this. He'd been yelling at them to stop, for Mr. Ormond to drop the gun and to let him go. Connor had been so afraid for his momma. She was lying so still and there was so much blood on her face and head. Mr. O had just pulled up his gun, pointed it at the policeman, and fired.

There had been so much blood then too. The man had just stopped moving and dropped to his knees. He had dropped so slowly like he couldn't believe that he'd been shot. But the hole in his head and the blood coming down his face made Connor know that he was dead. When he'd finally fallen to the floor, Mr. O had hit Connor with the gun and he didn't know anything else. Now here he was in the trunk of a car and didn't know if his momma was alive or not.

~~~

They were just eating some late night or early morning snack when Cait's phone started ringing. She got up from the table after looking at who might be calling. She went into the other room and it wasn't long before she was back. They all knew right away that something else had happened.

"One of my men was shot at the bus station about twenty minutes ago. They didn't call me sooner because they'd been trying to contact Tuck. Single gunshot wound to the head, DOA. It was Ormond and he has Connor and Charlie."

"Fuck! Are they all right? Did anyone see where they went? Damn it, I want them back here." Damon exploded.

"Damon, watch your mouth. But I quite agree we do need to get them back here. And soon. I've grown quite fond of that little boy and his mother. She was a perfect match for you too. Very nice young lady. We'll get her back. Cait, I want you to tell us what you know. Damon, do sit down. You're making me a nervous wreck. Pi, could you please make some of that nice tea of yours? Dane, sit. That baby will be born with colic if you don't settle down a bit. I swear, you children just don't know what to do when there's a crisis."

Damon leaned over and kissed his mother. She was gathering her troops and putting down the strategy. She would make a great commander in any type of war or in a large corporation. He loved his momma too.

"Charlie was seen being carried out over Ormond's shoulder and Connor was dragged out by his leg. Charlie had been knocked unconscious before my man was shot. I don't have a lot of details, but I'll get them for you. Connor was out when he was taken. I'm trying to get the tapes from the bus station now. I'm headed downtown to the station house."

Cait's phone rang again. This time, she didn't bother leaving the room and within a few seconds of listening, she sat down hard in the chair. When she looked up at Damon as she listened, he walked over to her and leaned his ear next to hers to listen.

"…everywhere. I've never seen so much blood, to tell you the truth. He had an entire set up in the basement— chains, leather, straps. We're still trying to find his trophies. I'm not sure why, but I got a feeling that they're here. We've called in the dogs to look at the yard, but it doesn't bode well for Ormond. With that much blood, there has to be at least two or more dead, we figure. I should have more for you in a couple of hours."

"How about his accounts? Have you had any luck in that area? My contact out here, another woman he may be holding, says that he had money. I want to be able to stop him here if at all possible. He took out one of my men today. He's going down here and I'm going to take him down." Cait said. She picked up a notebook that she had been using earlier and made a note on it. Captain Samuel Sanders—boss of Ormond. He is very cooperative now. Jackass. Raided his house two hours ago

"Sorry about your man. Hard to take when one of your own is taken for a senseless reason. Froze his accounts as of this morning. He won't be touching anything at this end. Money, though? Wasn't much in the bank, but the bedroom had over forty grand in it hidden around the room. It was the only room in the house that was clean, and I mean no blood in it," Captain Sanders said.

"Thanks. You've been a great deal of help. If there's anything else, will you please let me know?" Cait asked.

"You could let me come out there and help you arrest this bastard. He did some horrible things to some nice people out here. I'd like to be there if you think you can wait for me."

Cait looked at Damon and he shook his head. He didn't want to wait for anyone and especially someone that had to come all the way across the United States. She smiled at him and kissed his cheek.

"Can't do that, Sanders. This ass has two people that are very close to me and I'm not going to give him anymore time to hurt them. But if you leave right now, I'll let you in on the press conference when we catch him. I'll even make sure that they spell your name right in the papers."

"I'll hold you to that, Captain. I've got a seat out on the next flight to Columbus in about twenty minutes. I should be there in about three hours. I'll be the one with the crow pie in my hand."

Cait laughed. "I'll have an officer there to pick you up when you land and bring you to us. You know the rules when you come into my sandbox so I won't go into it. I'll see you in a few hours."

~~~

Charlie came awake slowly. She found that she was hanging from some sort of overhanging in a dark place. Her feet were tied to something heavy and her mouth was taped closed. Her body hurt in places she hadn't since she'd left Anthony. Trying to move, she realized that her leg was hurting very badly and she was sure it might be broken. And her head was pounding.

Straining as much as she could, Charlie tried to see if Connor was in the room with her and she couldn't see anyone. When she tried to stand up, she screamed behind the tape. Pain surged through her body like a knife. Breathing through her nose, she tried to control herself and work through the pain. It took everything she had to keep from letting the blackness take her. Connor needed her and she needed to figure out a way to get to him.

Bits and pieces of what had happened were coming back to her. The police officer had come up to them at the bus station. He was shouting for Anthony to drop the gun and to let the child go. He'd been saying something…something about her, but she couldn't remember what it had been. Her head started to pound more and she thought she might be sick. Breathing through her nose and trying to concentrate on not throwing up, she finally managed to get it under control.

Anthony had shot him, shot the poor policeman in the head. Screaming, she remembered the screaming around her. It occurred to her that she was the one screaming in addition to some of the people around her. Anthony kicked her soon after that. Connor. Connor had been hurt. His nose was bleeding and his mouth had been cut.

Anthony had done that too. The pain in her head was making her so ill she closed her eyes.

The next time she opened her eyes, there was more light in the area she was at. She could tell now that she was in some sort of box. It looked like she was in a trailer of a semi. There were holes in the side and it gave her enough light to see that she was tied to a cinderblock and that it was covered in blood. Her leg was broken. The bone was sticking out through her shin and it made her belly jump from the sight. Blood didn't pour from the wound, but there was a lot of blood around her. Bending her head, she looked up at her arms and could see that blood had dried on her arms.

Charlie was weak and she could barely stay off the broken leg. She tried to stand on the good leg, but it got to be too much too. Her arms were sore and the strain of having them tied above her head was pulling at her shoulders. She didn't have any idea how long she'd been there or how long Connor had been away from her, but she figured it had been a full day, if not longer. Crying again, she knew that even if Anthony came back right now, she'd not be able to do anything to him. She wouldn't be able to do anything at all to save her son. Charlie had failed Connor again.

And Damon. Charlie had failed him too. She'd never given him any chance to help her. She'd never given him any information that he and his family could have used to keep Anthony away and them safe. She'd just done what she always did, ran away. Crying harder now, she wished that she could do it all again. She'd tell Damon everything. Tell him that she wasn't worthy of him. She would also tell him that she loved him and that she always would.

Chapter 18

Connor could feel the car slow then stop. He was terrified that Mr. O was going to hurt him once the trunk opened. Picking up the gun again, he tried to figure out how to aim it. He didn't have any idea if he could shoot anybody, but he wasn't afraid to point it at someone. He had seen Mr. O use his gun. He seemed to just hold it and it would shoot whatever he aimed at. Connor didn't think it was that easy. If it was, Connor thought that everybody would be able to shoot perfectly.

The car was stopped now. There wasn't any more vibrating under him and the outside noises were quiet. When something scarped against where his head was, Connor nearly shouted out. When other noise started, like the sound of water being poured into the trunk, he started to panic. When nothing poured over him, he realized that Mr. O was putting gas in the car. Connor could hear him whistling now. Whistling some stupid country song that had been on the radio. Connor could hear how close he was to him. After a minute, Anthony started talking to him.

"You'll make not a single sound or I'll kill everyone at this station. And if that happens, brat, I'll make sure the police know that you were the one responsible for all their deaths. If they find out you did it, you get a life sentence for each person. Let's see, there is a woman putting gas in her van and I can see a little baby there. Oh, too bad about that. The courts hate when someone kills off a baby, especially when they're not even walking yet. There are two clerks in the store and then there's you. I'm going to enjoy killing you, brat. I'm going to take you back to your mother and then I'm going to blow your fucking head off while she watches."

Connor didn't say anything out loud, but inside he was screaming at Mr. O. Connor hadn't done anything other than go to the bathroom. Mr. O had come up behind Connor and banged his head against the urinal then slapped him hard across the mouth when he started to cry. Yanking his hair so hard that Connor saw stars, Mr. O had dragged him out of the bathroom and pointed at gun at his mother when he came out.

After Mr. O had shot the policeman, he'd walked over and started kicking Connor's momma. He'd kicked at her until Connor saw her leg break. When he'd seen the bone come through her skin, Connor threw up. He hadn't much on his stomach, but it was enough to make Mr. O stop hurting his mother and kick him. Connor didn't remember anything after that. He hoped that Mr. O would leave his momma there, but he was sure he didn't. Not after telling Connor that he planned to kill him in front of her.

When the car started up again and started to move, Connor pulled the gun closer to him and began to study it with his fingers and hands. He made sure he kept the barrel pointed away from himself at all times, but when the lid opened, he was going to be ready. He wasn't sure what he was going to be ready for, but he was going to be.

Connor had just put the gun on his chest when he felt the car start to slow again. Then it stopped altogether. He was sure that it couldn't be out of gas yet so he listened as hard as he could. Nothing. There were no sounds of other cars, no horns, and no more voices. When the door to the car squeaked open, Connor listened for Mr. O to come back to him. The sudden slamming of the car door had Connor jump. His heart started pounding hard in his little chest and a roaring started in his ears. He was sure that Mr. O had parked the car on a railroad track and was going to leave the car there for Connor to be killed. From not so far away, Connor heard a door shut, not like the car but like a house door. He didn't move. Connor lay there as tense as he'd ever been, waiting, just waiting for whatever Mr. O had planned. When the noise happened again, he jumped again.

The keys moving gave Connor a clue how close the man was. Then when Mr. O laughed, a giggle really, Connor picked up the gun. The scrape of the key in the lock had Connor pointing the gun up to where he thought someone would be standing. When the click opened the lock, Connor took a deep breath and held it. He was as ready as he'd ever be.

~~~

Damon paced the squad room. Charlie and Connor had been missing for over fifteen hours now and there had been nothing reported. Sanders was sitting in front of one of the many computers they had open, drinking coffee. There were several agents there now. By the time Sanders

171

had left Nevada and landed in Ohio, the dogs had uncovered three bodies buried in the back yard of Ormond's house. They were still looking and before it got too dark to dig, they'd found two more.

Cait had gone home about an hour ago. Spencer had told her if she didn't come home then he was coming there to get her. He'd tried the same threat on him, but Damon had just hung up on him. When his mother called ten minutes later, they'd gotten into a shouting match over the phone and then she'd hung up in tears. Damon looked up when there was a noise at the door. Byron and Devin were standing there looking as if they might want to go a couple of rounds with him. Damon thought that he could probably take them both on and win. He was so stressed out.

"Damon, can we have a word with you? Mom sent us to bring you home. She said you need to get some rest," Devin said when Damon walked over to see what the hell they wanted.

"No. I'm staying here. If someone calls in or they find them, I'm going to be here too. You can try to make me go, but I'm not going anywhere."

"We thought you'd say that. We'd do the same thing and we want you to know that. Jamie is picking up some food for everyone. We're going to stay here with you. Mom can just get over it. I'm going to deny that if you tell her I said it, but there you go." Devin pulled Damon into an embrace as he spoke.

Damon didn't know that he needed them until they got there. And the hugs were more than he expected. His family was everything to him, everything and more. When

Cait came over and hugged him too, Damon felt tears fill his eyes. For the first time in hours, Damon felt himself relax. Sitting down in one of the plastic chairs, he took a deep breath and closed his eyes. Ten minutes later, Jamie came in with pizza and another hug. After eating several slices of the gooey hot pizza, he leaned back and was asleep in seconds. His cell phone ringing woke him.

"Damon? It's Connor J. Kirkpatrick. I…I think I killed Mr. O. He shot me too and I think…I can't find my momma."

Damon was suddenly wide awake. His heart started pounding and it was all he could do to keep calm. He reached over to one of the desks near him and grabbed a pen. Scribbling out what was happening, he handed it to Jamie.

Connor shot. Says he shot Ormond. Charlie not w/him. Tell Cait.

To Connor, he started trying to get information. Out of the corner of his eye, he saw everyone stand to come to him. As they started giving him things to ask Connor, Damon turned to Devin, who immediately pushed everyone back.

"Connor, son, do you know where you are? Can you tell me anything that you can see so that we can come and get you? Anything, son, anything you can see, tell me."

He was quiet for a long time and Damon was terrified that something else had happened to him. Just when he was going to shout at him, Connor spoke up again. His voice was weak and he sounded like he was scared. Damon wanted to find the boy and hold him, pull him into his arms, and hold him for the next twenty years.

"We drove for a long time. He had to get gas. There's a house, but there ain't no phone in it. My momma's not in it either. I can't find her, Damon." Cait walked around her the men and handed Damon a list of questions she'd wrote down.

"You have to tell me where you are, Connor. I have to come and get you. Focus, son, tell me what you see. You said there was a house. Are there any numbers on it? Do you see a mail box? I want you to go and find a bedroom, see if there is a phone in there for me."

"I can't...he shot me and I can't...I'm in the living room, but I don't think I can go back outside again. I hurt too much. I'm sorry, Damon."

"Where are you shot, Connor? Tell me please. And where is Ormond? Is he in the house with you?"

"In my arm, in my left shoulder. There's a lot of blood and I'm dizzy. Mr. O is outside where I shot him. I was in the trunk and when he opened the thing up, I pulled the trigger. I know I hit him in the chest and I think in the neck, but I can't be sure. There was so much blood and I hurt so bad. Damon, I don't want to die."

"I don't want you to die either, Connor. Do you still have the gun on you? If you do, do you remember how many times you pulled the trigger?"

"No, I dropped it. I think...it might be in the trunk or on the ground. Okay, I'm in the bedroom. I can't...I'm so dizzy, Damon. Do you know where my momma is? I wanted a puppy, but Mr. O wouldn't let me have one. I'm so tired."

"Connor! You can't go to sleep. I need for you to stay with me. Is there a phone there? Can you see one? Connor?"

It was a long time this time. Five minutes passed before Connor spoke again and Damon was frantic with worry. He couldn't get to him and he didn't know where he was. When Connor came back on the line, he sounded much weaker and Damon was extremely worried.

"I have the phone. It's...blue. I never saw a blue phone before. I know I have to do something for you, but I can't remember what it was. I'm so tired. Let me take...I want to take a little nap. Okay?"

"Connor, please stay with me. Your momma needs you to stay awake. I want you to dial zero for me. Can you do that? Dial zero and talk to the operator. Connor? Are you listening to me?"

"Yes. Zero. I can do that. But I can't talk to her. I can't stay awake anymore. You find my momma and you tell her that I killed the bastard...tell her I love her."

Damon couldn't get Connor to answer him anymore no matter how many times he shouted at him. Cait came over and told him that they had a nine-one-one call in from a town just outside of London, Ohio and that squads were on the way to the address. Their ETA was three minutes. Damon never stopped talking to Connor, begging him to please come to the phone and speak to him. Five minutes after he spoke to Cait, the EMTs came on the line. Their news wasn't encouraging.

~~~

Charlie couldn't stand, not even on her good leg, and her arms were numb. The light that had been coming

175

through the walls was dimmer now and she couldn't see as well. It didn't matter, nothing had changed anyway. No Connor, no Damon. She was alone.

There were sounds around her, just outside the container where she was. The sound of trucks, some heavy, others not so large, rambled by her. Once she thought she heard a helicopter, but couldn't be sure. Things were beginning to not make a lot of sense to her.

Most of her thoughts centered on Connor and Damon. She wanted to see them again. Charlie couldn't be sure, but she thought she was dying. There was something so final in the way her mind accepted that. She knew that Damon would care for Connor and raise him to be a good, upstanding young man. She also knew that he would have benefits that she'd never have been able to provide for him. Her heart hurt at that thought.

Charlie thought of her mother too. She'd not spoken to her in years, not since she'd thrown her out when she'd refused to have an abortion. Charlie wondered if she would be proud of her or Connor and decided it didn't matter. Then there was Connor's father. He'd never even seen his son and Charlie was sad for that too. She'd of course told Connor how he'd been conceived. She had even told him his father's name, though it wasn't on the birth certificate. His family had threatened her in ways she didn't like to think about now.

The bright light woke her the next time. And the noise. When she tried to pull away from them both, the pain nearly overwhelmed her again. The voices were saying things. She couldn't make them out, but the one she heard more than the others was Dane's.

"Connor?" Charlie almost didn't recognize her own voice. It was harsh and rough. Her lips felt so dry and she was sure that they didn't fit her face anymore. The picture of her with giant lips entered her mind and she giggled at the thought.

"Charlie? Can you hear me? I need you to answer me, sweetheart. Can you hear me? Connor is in the hospital. He needs you. You have to stay with me, all right? Charlie?"

Connor was hurt? Charlie's fuzzy mind tried to work around that, but all she could manage was pain. Her arms were on fire and she could hear screaming again. She wanted to tell the person, she thought it was Dane, to shut up, but her lips didn't fit anymore. Then she was fading, fast and hard through a plethora of colors and memories. Damon. Connor. Margaret and the others. As she let the blackness take her, she realized she was moving.

Chapter 19

Damon looked down at the woman lying in the bed. Even with her being so pale and her lips cracked and split, she was still the most beautiful creature he'd ever seen. The doctor who had operated on her had told them that she had lost a great deal of blood, not only from the break in her leg, but from the beating she'd gotten later. Her back and torso were badly bruised in addition to being cut up.

The break in her leg was compound. Ormond had kicked her so many times that he'd broken her femur bone in three places. The orthopedic surgeon had had to reinforce the shattered bone with steel rods and said that Charlie may need additional surgery later to ensure that the bone was strong enough. But he assured them all that with proper care, she wouldn't lose her leg. Damon planned to make sure she got excellent care. The little boy in the bed beside him stirred.

When the EMTs had said that the news about their patient wasn't good, they weren't referring to Connor. Anthony had been shot twice, once near the heart, just missing the aortic artery by centimeters, and once in the neck. Connor had missed that artery by a lesser margin than he had Ormond's heart. He was now in intensive care with round the clock security. Ormond was also cuffed to his bed by his legs and his wrists.

Connor had fared better than anyone. His gunshot wound was in his shoulder and had broken his collar bone. He wouldn't have any lasting effects of the injury. He would only need to go through some physical therapy to get it back into shape. He had lost a lot of blood, but once they got him hooked up to an IV and pushed the fluids, he'd been better in no time. He was still recuperating and had only just today been moved to his mother's room to be nearer to her.

"Has Momma waked up yet? I miss her. I want her to talk to me." Damon knew the kid missed her. Damon did too.

"No. But the doctor said it takes a while for the trauma to heal. You know she's only going to yell at you when she finds out what you did. I'm sure she'll hug you, but she's going to be pissed too."

"I don't care so long as she wakes up to do it. I'll let her yell at me all she wants to. Heck, she can even ground me like Mrs. P said she was gonna do to Momma when she woke up. I don't know what she'll take from me, but she sure can do it." Connor grinned and rolled back over and closed his eyes. He was sleep within minutes. Damon had to grin as well. He was such a great kid.

Connor had told them what had happened once he had been taken from the bus station. When he'd heard the trunk open, he'd been ready to defend himself against whatever happened. And he had. Anthony had been ready to find him cowering in the trunk and must have been surprised to be met with an eight-year-old toting a nine millimeter.

"You'll back away from me, you old bastard. I ain't afraid to shoot you. You tell me where my momma's at right now," Connor had told the older man when he started to reach in.

"Where the hell did you get that? Give me that right now before you hurt someone. I don't know who you think you are, but you never draw a weapon on a cop, kid. Now hand it over."

When he'd lunged for the gun, Connor fired. He'd told the police that he hadn't meant to shoot Mr. O. But he'd been so afraid that he must have pulled the trigger. As Anthony staggered back, he'd fired at Connor. The bullet went wild and had ended up hitting window in the back of the car and shattering it. Connor moved, trying to get out of the trunk and away from Ormond, but the man wouldn't stay down.

"You fucking brat. I'm going to kill you for this. Look what you've done. You've shot me in the chest. If I die from this, I'm going to beat you to death."

Connor told the police that he couldn't believe the stupid man said that, but Connor said he'd been saying stupid crap for a long time. When Ormond had raised his gun to fire at Connor again, Connor ducked down behind the lip of the trunk and that shot missed too.

"I was afraid to lift my head again, so I just rested the gun on the trunk and started pulling the trigger. I heard Mr. O screaming at me to stop it. I think he really thought I would too. I think he thought I'd be like, 'oh sorry, did I hurt you? Well let me give you my gun.' Stupid bastard. When the gun kinda came apart and wouldn't fire no more, I threw it at him and waited. I must have taken a nap or something 'cause when I woke up, it was almost dark outside. I got out and that's when I realized he'd shot me. I know he was shooting back at me, but I didn't feel nothing until I woke up."

"Then what did you do, Connor? Where did you get the phone to call Damon?" one of the agents asked him. Connor looked over at Cait, and at her nod, he continued.

"I took it off him, Mr. O. It was just laying there in his hand and I needed to get me some help. I didn't steal it. I swear I was going to give it back to him, but I went into the house to call zero like Damon told me to and I fell asleep again."

"You didn't fall asleep, Connor. You'd lost a lot of blood and you were in shock. Your body shut down to rest and to start to heal up. No one thinks you stole the phone. You did really well. Now tell us what happened next."

Cait glared at the agents sitting next to Connor's bed as she hurried to reassure him. It was everything Damon could do not to burst out laughing. Cait could make a grown man wet himself with one of her glares and these two men were quickly learning that.

"I could see that Mr. O was bleeding real bad. I didn't want to get close, but I had to get the phone. His gun was there and I started to move it out of his hand when he grabbed me around the neck. I had his gun so I hit him with it. I heard his nose crunch and when he let me go, I jumped back and fell down. His gun just pulled the trigger all by itself. I didn't even have my finger on the trigger thing or nothing. This bullet hit him in the neck. He grabbed at it, but it was bleeding real bad. I didn't stay there. He might have had another gun, so I took off to the other side of the car and waited. Then I called Damon. He told me to go in the house and call the police. I was really tired again and fell asleep on the floor. I don't remember nothing else until I woke up here and Damon was sitting next to me."

Devin came in as they were taking Charlie's blood pressure later that morning. He simply sat down and stared at the nurse while she finished up. Damon knew his brother well enough to know that he'd get to whatever was on his mind eventually, so Damon waited.

"Connor is a really great kid, you know that? I think what he did to save himself is perhaps the bravest thing I've ever heard. Ronnie wants to give him shooting lessons. Think his mother will go for that?"

"I don't know. I think I'd wait a while to ask her. She's going to freak out enough just knowing that he shot someone with one. She might come around, but it might take her a year or two."

Devin only nodded. Damon leaned forward and took Charlie's hand into his. In the five days she'd been in the hospital, she looked better. Her lips were soft again because Damon made sure that they were covered in moisture wear lip cover three times a day. The bruise on her face was fading too. The swelling in her eye was down and almost normal again. When Devin spoke this time, Damon didn't even bother turning around.

"Ormond is suing Connor. He doesn't have a case, of course, but he is accusing Connor of attempted murder.

Taylor knows of the attorney and said that he'd try his own mother if there was a dime in it. I don't think it'll go to court, but Jamie and Dane have said they'd post his bail. I'm kinda hoping it will go to trial. Could be kind of fun trying a case that is so stupid."

Damon laughed out loud. He could see it now. "Mass murderer sues eight-year-old because he fought back—news at eleven." Damon glanced over at Connor and was relieved to see he was still asleep.

"I'd like you to keep this to yourself, please. I think they've both got enough to worry about right now. Tell me what else is on your mind, Devin. You didn't just come here to tell me about this."

Devin was quiet for a little while longer and when he spoke again, Damon turned sharply to look at him. This wasn't what he had expected at all.

"Connor's dad contacted me yesterday afternoon. He said that he wants to see his son and that he'd been looking for him for some time. He is claiming that Charlie has been keeping them apart."

"You don't believe that, do you? Or him? Shit! Why now? Why now, after eight years, does he want to see his son? What did you tell him?"

"I told him that he'd have to have a DNA test done and once we got the results of that back, we'd work from there. I pulled Connor's birth certificate and the father's name is listed as 'unknown.' Did Charlie ever tell you anything about Connor's dad?"

"He ain't my dad. Momma said he's was just the sperm donor. He raped her one night 'cause he wanted to brag to the other kids he'd had the ice queen. But Momma wasn't a queen of nothing. You make him stay away from me, Uncle Devin. I don't want nothing to do with him."

Connor sat up in the bed and regarded them both. Damon was a little pissed at Devin for bringing it up now, and more mad at himself because he hadn't stopped him. Devin didn't look all that happy either.

"Connor, he has a right to see you if he wants to. We can slow him down with paper work, but in the end, unless he gave up those rights before you were born, then he can see you. He can even demand that you see him," Devin started to explain.

"He did. He signed one of those papers when Momma told him she was pregnant. I seen it. She has it in a safety vault at the bank. She has all kinds of stuff that he mailed her when she wouldn't kill me. And some stuff that he sent her after she wouldn't give me up for adoption. She told me that she was keeping it in case he decided to come back and claim me when I became famous and rich. That man's momma even came to see me one day. She said I was a bondable...abdominal...she said I wasn't right."

Connor was crying now so Damon went to the bed and picked him up. He looked at Devin and was ready to blast him good when he noticed that Charlie was looking at them. Damon turned Connor's face toward his mother and waited.

"Abomination. She called you an abomination. You're not. You're my little boy." Then she closed her eyes again.

Connor and Damon looked at each other and started laughing. Soon Devin joined them. She had woken up. Charlie had woke up and spoke to them.

~~~

Two days later, Charlie opened her eyes again. She looked around the room and was surprised by all the pretty flowers everywhere. And the variety of them as well. She was trying to look at them all when she noticed Damon and Connor asleep, Damon in a large chair and Connor in a hospital bed.

"They haven't left this room since you were brought in nine days ago. How are you feeling, sweetheart? You look much better than you did when they brought you in."

Charlie looked over at the woman sitting in the big chair on the other side of the bed. Charlie noticed that she had a book on her lap and a laptop on the arm of the chair. Margaret Parker looked right at home sitting there with her hair styled, beautiful silk blouse, twill pants, and bright green frog slippers on her feet.

"Frogs?" It hurt to talk and Charlie had to work to make each word come out. But apparently, Margaret understood her because she wiggled her feet.

"Jacob gave me these for Christmas last year. I think they're a little much, but they are warm. Little Jim gave me a matching robe. It even has a cap on it that comes up over my head and has these big eyes. I understand it was a fight to see who gave me the robe and Little Jim won. You didn't answer me, dear, how are you feeling?"

"Hurt. Thirsty, too. Connor all right? He's okay?" She did hurt, too, but nothing like she did before.

"Yes. He's perfectly fine. He's a wonderful boy. You've done a very good job raising him."

"Thank you. You too, with Damon. Love him. Very much." Charlie felt the tears fill her eyes and started to look away when she saw Margaret stand and pull a tissue from the nearby box. As she wiped away Charlie's tears, she sniffled too.

"I love all of my children, Charlie, including you. Connor has asked to call me grandma. I hope you don't mind, but I told him yes. You know, for some reason, having someone call you grandma because they're related to you and having one call you that because they love you feels very different. I've never been prouder. Now. We need to talk about your wedding."

Charlie must have looked like a deer in head lights because that's what she felt like. Wedding? Charlie glanced over at Damon and then back at his mother. She didn't even know if Damon still wanted to marry her or not.

"Well, of course he does. Don't be a dolt. I think we can have everything planned for Valentine's Day. Ben, Taylor's mother, said he would design your dress for you. He thinks you should have something in cream with red trim. Said it would go nicely with your coloring. Of course there are the bridesmaid dresses—you'll want the girls as those, won't you?"

"Too much. Slow down, please. Damon wants to marry me still?" Charlie looked over at Damon again and noticed that he and Connor both were awake. Neither of them made a move to come and rescue her, she noticed.

"Yes, Damon still wants to marry you, Charlie. And he would be very happy if his mother would let his future wife plan at least a small part of her wedding. Connor, why don't you take your pushy grandmother down to the cafeteria and let her buy you a drink? I need to speak to your mom."

"Okay, Damon. Grandma, come on. I'm betting he wants to kiss her or something gross like that. That's all the guys do, isn't it? Kiss all over the girls. How do they stand it?" Connor was pulling Margaret out the door as he asked.

"He'll need a talk about the birds and the bees soon. I think we should let Nicky do it. He told me about them when I was nine. I couldn't eat for a week much less touch a girl. Well, not until I was eleven or so. Sally Handle…ah there's a fine memory. She was the one who taught me…well, that's for another time. How are you?"

Charlie looked up at him as he came toward her. All sorts of thing were running through her mind and none of them had anything to do with how she felt, but more on the birds and the bees.

"Fine. You?" Damon's grin made her body stir. She had a cast on her leg from the bottom of her foot to the top of her thigh, she hadn't brushed her hair or her teeth in over a week, and she was wearing a hospital gown made of the thinnest cotton known to man and the ugliest shade of puce she'd ever seen.

"Better now that you're awake. I was so worried about you. And scared. I have to tell you this now because I don't want you to think that I'm okay with you leaving me, but you are so going to get your ass whipped. I think I might have to do it several times to make sure you understand that running is no longer an option."

Damon's voice had turned to silk, but she could still hear the steel in it. He wanted her to know he meant business, but at the same time that he was going to make her enjoy whatever punishment he wielded out as much has she did. She could hardly wait.

"Anthony won't stop. He'll keep coming until we're dead. He hates Connor. I have to protect him."

"We have to protect him. And Anthony is going to prison as soon as his trial is over. He's been caught. He killed six women that we know of in Nevada and some that the police might not be able to find. They found about forty trophies in his house. But enough about him, let's talk about you and me. We'll have a huge wedding. About five hundred guests and maybe twice that for the reception. Valentine's is fine with me so long as you live with me until then."

Charlie laughed at Damon. She hoped that she could be there when he informed his mom that Charlie was going to live with him before the wedding. While Margaret wasn't a prude, she did have rules she liked followed. And living together was one of those rules.

Chapter 20

Dane was sitting in the chair five days later when she came back from x-ray. The pregnant woman looked like she was having a good time watching some sort of game show on the room's television. Her laughter could be heard down the hall.

"Pi watches these things like it's her job. I can see the fun in it, but not the why. People are very strange, are they not? I've come to see how things are going. I was told not to ask you how you feel. I guess that's a sort of touchy subject for you."

Charlie was going to snap if one more person inquired about her health. She was fine. She was in a hospital with a broken leg and other injuries, not at home with a cold. Poor Byron had gotten the brunt of that little hissy fit when he'd inquired after her yesterday.

"I didn't mean to take it out on Byron. He was just...he was just there. Is he mad at me?" Charlie wouldn't blame him if he was. She'd yelled at him for a good ten minutes before he left. A dozen roses had shown up an hour later from him, but he hadn't been back.

"No. He told me to tell you that he left because he was afraid that if you caught him laughing, you might have hurt him. Byron has the best sense of humor of anyone I know. I think it's because he's the middle child or thereabouts. No, he doesn't anger easily. I've come to talk to you about some things. Are you up to being quiet until I finish?"

Charlie was sure she wasn't going to like this conversation any more than the one she'd had with Devin earlier. She'd had to give him a signed affidavit to get into her safety deposit box at her bank in Nevada. Charlie couldn't believe that Connor's dad, Brody Gibbons, was trying to sue her for joint custody after all these years. And claiming that she hadn't told him about Connor.

"I suppose. Did all you women become bossy when you married the Grants, or is it just natural to you? I don't much care for it myself."

Instead of being insulted, Dane laughed. She leaned over as best she could, pulled out a box, and laid it on the edge of the bed. It was a laptop. When Dane stood and began pulling other things out of the bag, she continued speaking.

"I think it's necessary for us to be bitchy. If we didn't, I doubt the men would let us leave the house without police escort. All of us are much stronger than they give us credit for. You'll learn. This is a gift from Jamie and me and before you get your panties all twisted up, you need to know that as you work for me, you'll need to keep track of my incoming emails and other things. It's loaded with everything and there is a printer for you at the house. I've also downloaded a scheduler for me. That way you can keep track of stuff I have to take care of so I'm not overworked. You won't be either."

Charlie could see that. She wasn't happy about the comment concerning her panties, but decided to let it go for now. As Dane explained things, she set up the computer and plugged it in.

"This cell phone is yours too. I think it has everything too, though I'm not sure how it works yet. You play with it here and we'll go over what we don't understand next time we can go out together. I have one just like it. Jamie programmed in all the phone numbers and there's a list of them here in this folder. The phone number is here too. I'm not sure, but I think you should get one for Connor too. Maybe not this fancy, but you can figure it out."

Charlie looked at the phone. She'd never had a cell phone before and wondered who on earth she'd call on it. She didn't say anything, just laid it beside her as Dane handed her another folder.

"Devin is the family attorney with his wife Ronnie. I know you've been told about this Gibbons person and Connor so I won't go into my opinion of his sorry ass. But Devin thought you might want to look this over. He flew out to Nevada to get your stuff from the bank this morning. He said that he'll be in to talk to you tomorrow. This is the information he gathered on Gibbons."

Charlie opened the file and looked at the first picture. She hadn't seen Brody in nine years and they hadn't been good to him. For a reason she didn't want to think about, she was actually happy about that. Turning to the next page, there was a newspaper clipping that had a picture of Connor and her at the charity event. They were standing next to Damon and Dane. Charlie read the caption under the picture.

"Society is out in full swing tonight in all their finery. Damon Grant with date, Charlotte Kirkpatrick, and son Connor, are seen here with billionaire Dane Grant just before the gala began. Rumor has it that Ms. Kirkpatrick is engaged to the millionaire doctor."

"That ran in all the papers the next afternoon. Ronnie thinks that's why this Gibbons person is trying to get with Connor now after all this time. He smells money. If you read the report on him, it seems this man has been down on his luck for some time. He also had three other children that he's reportedly the father of too."

Charlie looked up at Dane. She couldn't think past the caption. Dane was a billionaire and Damon a millionaire? Shit!

"I don't...that is, I...don't have...you're a billionaire? You seem so...I don't know...regular. I mean, you don't seem like a snob at all. That didn't come out right either. What I meant was—"

"It's okay, Charlie, I know what you mean. I do have a great deal of money, but I'm still just plain old Dane Grant. I'd much rather have my grandmother back than all the money, but she made sure I was well provided for. My mother and I never got along either, so you and I have that in common. You'll find that we all have something to relate to one another with."

The two women talked about Gibbons for a little while longer then about the upcoming holiday. Dane gave Charlie a credit card and showed her how to set up an account to order on line.

"The card is yours. Don't say anything about it, all right? Consider it an advance on your pay checks. You'll have to order your Christmas online or find what you want so just pay for it and when you come to work, we'll work out a payment schedule for it. If you order something locally, one of us will pick it up for you, otherwise have things sent to my house. I promise not to peek in the boxes."

Christmas. Charlie hadn't thought of buying gifts for anyone. When she started to say that she didn't have a clue what to get the new people in her life, Dane saved her again.

"Here is a list of stuff the kids want. The things we've already gotten are marked out. I know it's a bit overwhelming, but it's a lot of fun. We go to Margaret's house for Christmas Eve and open gifts on Christmas morning. Damon said you might be out by then."

"The doctor said maybe Christmas day. I don't know what to say. Thanks seems so...it seems so inadequate. You've, all of you have been so nice to Connor and I. I don't know if I'll ever be able to repay you." Charlie could feel the tears threatening again and turned away.

"You just make Damon happy. That's all we want. He's the greatest man I know, well, besides James. But you keep making him smile and laugh and that'll be payment enough for all of us."

Dane left a little while later. She said the baby was really making her tired a lot and wanted to take a much needed nap before Jamie got home from class. Charlie settled back in the bed and began her shopping. It was the most fun she'd had in ages.

~~~

Three weeks later on Christmas Eve morning, Charlie got to go home. She still had the cast on and would for several more weeks. Then there was the hurt ribs still mending but much better. But everyone was thrilled to have her home. Connor hardly left her side all morning long and Charlie needed a break. She smiled at Damon when he walked in.

"Connor, Byron is here. Tell your mom bye and get out of here. And remember what I told you."

"Yes, sir. Bye, Momma. Have a good nap." Then he was gone.

Charlie looked at Damon. "I'm back now and while I appreciate you keeping an eye on him the past month, I think I should take over his care now. Please don't take this the wrong way, but I—"

"Don't say it then. Because I can see what's brewing on your face and it will piss me off. I didn't come up here to fight with you."

"Then why did you come up here? Connor and I were having a perfectly good day and you sent him off. And there was nothing brewing on my face." Charlie blushed. She blushed because she was "brewing," as he'd put it. And though she was glad for the reprieve, Connor was still her son.

"I came up here because we have the house to ourselves for the next few hours. I came up here because I want to make love to you. It's been a very lonely month without you in my bed. I came up here to see if I could persuade you to let me taste you, make you come in my mouth. I thought I'd make you scream again."

Charlie's body heated at his words. Her pussy wept for his mouth, his cock, anything that he wanted to touch her with. She had to press her thighs together or embarrass herself by reaching down and touching herself.

"I…what about my cast? I think…it'll be in the way, won't it? Damon, I don't think that we should try anything like that. I mean it's…I have a cast on my leg."

"Yes, I can see that. But it's not your leg I want to taste. Open your legs for me, Charlie. Let me see if you missed me as much as I missed you."

Charlie had no control over her body. Her thighs parted as if he were pulling them apart. When she stopped with them just a few inches open, he moved the skirt of her dress up further and pressed his hands between her legs and pushed them wider. She watched his hands skim up her legs and back down. Her moan was out before she could stop it. She pressed her hand over her mouth.

"Never hold back when we make love, Charlie. I want to hear your enjoyment. I want to know that you are enjoying me touch you, making love to you, or anything else I do to you as much as I do. Are you wet, baby? Are your juices soaking your panties? Let me see, let me feel you."

When his finger moved up her thighs and then to her hips, she moaned again, this time not trying to mask what she was feeling. His hands were hot on her skin and when he ran his fingers up under the sides of her panties and started to pull them off, she lifted herself up so that he could get them off easier. When he stood next to the bed with her panties in his hand, she watched as he put them to his nose and inhaled deeply.

"Heaven. You smell like heaven to me. I want to strip naked and bury myself deep into your hot pussy, but I know that it'll hurt you right now. So as much as I hate to do it, I'm going to hold off at least for a couple more days getting naked anywhere near you. But I want to see you, all of you. Unbutton your dress and take it off. I want to watch you strip for me."

Charlie reached for the buttons on her dress and began working them through the tiny holes. She didn't take her eyes off Damon as she did it. When he took off his belt and undid his pants, she wanted to shout for him to hurry. As Damon reached into his briefs and freed his cock, she licked her lips.

"I'm going to come like this. Right now, I'm not sure if I'll make it until you're completely bare for me, but I'm going to try. I want to come all over your breasts. I want to see my cum on your nipples. Hurry, love. I'm so close to exploding now that I'm hurting."

"Give me your cock, Damon. I want you to come down my throat, please? I want to suck you off."

Damon stepped forward and when he was close enough for her to touch, she ran her thumb over his tip, gathered the stream of cum already gathering there, and put it into her mouth. He growled at her and her pussy flooded the sheets beneath her. Pulling his cock closer, she swiped her tongue over the tip and tasted him. Spicy, hot, and salty, she closed her mouth over him and swirled around the fat head. His gentle rock into her mouth became harder and a little less controlled with each pass of her tongue.

"Christ, Charlie! That's it, baby. Suck me. Jesus, I'm not going to last. I've been thinking about tasting that sweet pussy of your for a week now and I can't believe I'm not going to…that's it, Charlie, oh baby, I'm coming. Shit!"

The first surge of his cum hitting her tongue made her reach between her legs and press against her clit. The harder he pumped into her mouth, the harder she fucked herself with her fingers. When he jerked away from her, his cum still pulsing from him and splashed across her breast, Charlie screamed out her release. Hot liquid covered her and she reached up with both her hands and rubbed it into her nipples and breasts.

When Damon lifted her good leg up and pressed it against his chest, he entered her. With his thick cock and the feeling of him deep inside of her, she came again. This time, with is cock deep inside of her, she felt her climax all the way to her head. He filled her and when he stiffened, he reached down and pinched her clit hard and brought her to peak again as she felt his cum fill her, heat her from the inside out.

He slowly lowered her leg and gently rolled off her. Sweat and his cum covered her body, but she didn't mind either feeling. When he was on his back, he lay there for several moments, his breathing harsh. She couldn't help but smile.

"I thought you said you weren't going to do that. Next time you don't want to do that again, let me know. That was wonderful. I'm almost afraid to think how well you'll do when you want to do that."

His laughter burst from him and he pulled her closer to him. She could still feel her heart pounding in her chest and closed her eyes with the deepest sense of completion. It wasn't long before she was drifting off to sleep.

Chapter 21

Damon woke to his phone ringing. It took him several seconds to realize why he was naked and alone in the bed. Then he heard the toilet flush and smiled at what had happened. Charlie was just making her way back to the bed with her crutches when he opened his phone. It was his mom.

"I do hope Charlie is relaxing. Poor girl must be worn completely out. You make sure you take good care of her today so that she'll be able to come over for Christmas tomorrow, all right?"

"I've been taking very good care of her, Mom. And I don't think I've ever seen her so relaxed. I plan to take very good care of her as much as she'll let me today."

Damon threw off the sheet and stroked his cock while Charlie watched him. It was hard as stone and he wanted her in the worst way. He'd forgotten about his mom on the phone when she asked what was wrong when he groaned.

"Nothing. Charlie needs me and I was getting up. Why don't I call you later, Mom? I want to help Charlie back to bed, all right?"

"Yes, all right. But Damon, I'm telling you right now, there had better be a long wait between your marriage and another baby from you two. It's not that I won't love another grandchild, but this hurrying to the altar is getting to be old hat."

"But Mom, sex is so much fun this way. I love you. I'll talk to you later." He hung up while she was still sputtering and turned to Charlie. "Come here, love. I never got to taste you earlier and I am desperate to do so now."

"Did you just tell your mother that we're having sex? Like right now having sex? I don't believe you. How will I ever be able to face her again without thinking about that?"

Charlie hadn't moved, but that didn't matter to him. Damon eased off the bed and went to her. His cock jerked when he was close enough to touch her. Dropping down to his knees, he ran his fingers up her thighs and then slid one into her heat.

"Charlie, will you be able to stand up on your crutches while I eat you? If not, tell me now because I plan to make a full meal of you. You're so wet, love. And tight."

"Damon, please. I don't think we should...yes!" Charlie hissed out her approval when he touched the sweet spot inside of her.

Charlie's body shuddered when he pushed another finger inside. She was soaking his hand with her juices and he leaned forward and licked her slit until her little nub found its way clear of her nether lips. Damon suckled it into his mouth and worried it with his tongue. When she started to tilt, he pulled back and stood up.

"Can't have you fall over. Let me put you to bed so that we can both enjoy this. That's it, baby, lie down and let me do all the work."

Damon

When he had Charlie in the center of the bed, he put a pillow under her leg and moved it as far over as he could without hurting her. He'd thought of nothing else but having this woman, thought of nothing else but claiming her and making love to her for weeks. As much as he wanted to be inside of her, the need to taste was stronger. Damon laid down between her open legs and began fucking her with his fingers.

"You're so tight here. I love to feel your walls pull at me when I'm deep inside of you. The way you milk my cock when you come is like nothing I've ever felt before."

"Please stop talking and take me. I want to feel your mouth on me, Damon. Just shut up and do it."

Damon didn't want to disappoint her so using both his hands, he opened her nether lips and sucked her clit into his mouth. Charlie came immediately, bucking and riding his mouth, nearly throwing him off in the process. Moving his mouth down to her opening, he began lapping her juices with his tongue. Hot, spicy cum filled his mouth and slid down his throat. He drank from her and when she began to slow her movements, he pressed two of his fingers deep inside of her as he continued to taste her. Damon slid his tongue over the most sensitive flesh of her woman's body and exulted in her ragged moan as she poured into him. His tongue moved further into her, then out again, mimicking the rhythm of sex while he clasped the firm flesh of her ass in his hands to pull her closer and closer still.

Never had anyone's pleasure brought him so much happiness. Her body responded naturally to his. And when he felt her tighten around his fingers again, he nipped at her clit and had her coming apart again.

"Please, Damon. Please, I want to feel you inside of me again. I want to feel you come in me again, fill me with you. Please." Begging him so prettily, he moved to do what she wanted. With his cock at her entrance, he paused and looked down at her.

"Charlie, I didn't use a condom before and I don't want to now either. I love the feeling of your heat wrapping around me. The feeling of my cum pouring deep into you. We may create a child tonight. Are you all right with that?"

Charlie looked up at him, wide-eyed. He couldn't tell what was going through her mind, but he hoped that she wouldn't turn him away. He wanted her to want him this way.

"You want a baby with me? You want me to get pregnant, Damon? You want me to carry your baby?"

"More than anything in this world. I want to watch you grow large with one. I want to feel it move as it grows. I can't wait to see you having our child, love. I love Connor very much and will always think of his as my own, but to see you swollen with our child makes me want for things I've never known before."

Charlie looked at him for a long moment. His cock ached to be deep within her heat, but he wouldn't rush her. Not about this, never about something like this.

"Yes. Please, I want to have your baby. I want that too. I never thought that I would...I never thought I'd ever...please, Damon, give me your baby."

He slammed into her hard and deep. Knowing that he was bare within her made him want to…no, need to come hard and fast. Her leg wrapped around his hip and he held her in place as he rocked deep within her. When Charlie arched up off the bed, he leaned over her and nipped her nipple and filled her.

~~~

Christmas morning was beautiful. There had been a light dusting of snow on the ground when Connor had come home and sometime during the night, two inches had fallen. Connor had never seen snow, not like this, and he had wanted to go out and play in it as soon as he'd eaten his breakfast.

"Don't you want to open your gifts? I know you don't believe in Santa, but there are a few things under the tree for you, kiddo. Come on and we'll take a peek."

Dane had brought Charlie's gifts over the day before she'd come home from the hospital. They had been wrapped, Charlie saw, and was thrilled to see what Connor would think about what she'd gotten him. And what she'd gotten Damon, though his would have to be opened later, in private.

Charlie had gotten Connor a computer. It had taken her almost three days of worrying about it before she'd made the purchase. Of course she'd talked to Damon about it first. She didn't know if he'd be all right with Connor needing to have the Internet hooked up or not. She grinned when she remembered the small fight they'd had about the house and that it belonged to her as much as him. The next day he'd brought in the deed for her to sign.

Damon had put her name on it right along with his. She now owned half a house.

"Now I don't want to hear another word about my house," he'd told her. "It's our house, as are the car and the truck. Half of everything I own, you now own too. Your name is on the checking account, the credit cards, and everything else we now own. Got it?"

"Yes. But it wasn't necessary to get it done before we're married. I could have waited until then to have the house in my name too."

"Maybe you could, but I couldn't. Now sign the damned papers so I can get them back to Devin before he has a shit fit. He said I should have done this a week ago. I told him I just got you in my bed. I wasn't going to go throwing legal papers at you just then."

When Connor opened the box and saw what it was, he nearly knocked the tree over getting to her to hug her. Even after he opened his other gifts, and he had a lot of them, she noticed that he kept touching the computer box. Charlie had never been able to give him anything before when they'd lived with Anthony and this had felt wonderful.

"Now, for you, Momma. I got you something too. Byron helped me get it. And then Ronnie helped me pick out the...well, you open it."

Charlie's fingers trembled when she started peeling the tape off the pretty paper. When Connor growled at her and took it from her, he ripped open the wrapping and handed her the framed picture. It was of him.

The picture was of him standing next to a large tree. He had on his jacket and his head was bare so she could see the huge smile on his face when he looked at the camera. The colors were wonderful, Connor's shirt was a deep blue, and his jacket was a tan color. His dark jeans and heavy boots against the light dusting of snow made him look rugged and tough. She gently ran her finger down his face in the picture as tears fell down her cheeks.

"Ah Momma, don't cry. If you don't like it, Aunt Morgan said you could pick out another picture. She must have taken about three hundred that day. She said you'd like this one best 'cause is shows off my manly features. I don't know what she meant by that, but I just nodded. Sometimes I think it's easier than letting her explain stuff to me. She gets all weepy when she does it. Uncle Nicky said it was gourmands. I don't know what that is either, but he seemed okay with it."

"I think he meant hormones, but yes, pregnant women have that problem. I love this, Connor. It's the most perfect picture of you I've ever seen. I'm going to put it in my bedroom and look at it every day. Thank you."

Charlie hugged the picture to her chest and watched as Connor finished opening his gifts. She and Damon had gone overboard and she didn't care. He needed so much and the best was yet to come. The week after he started school in January, Connor was having his room redecorated.

"Okay, now it's my turn. I got you something practical. I know that you said not to get you anything, but that was just not going to fly with me. Here." Damon handed her a small box.

Charlie tried to open it the same way she had Connor's, but again, it was taken from her and the paper ripped away. Didn't these guys want to savor anything? She flushed slightly when she remembered Damon and the way he had savored her yesterday and again last night. When she looked up at him when he gave her back the box, she realized he remembered to. He leaned close to her ear and whispered to her.

"You keep looking at me like that and Connor will be going to Mom's without us. Open the damned box so that I can kiss you."

This time, the trembling of her fingers had nothing to do with happiness but with need. The things Damon could do to her with only a few words. A set of keys spilled out into her hand.

"It's a big car, Mom! Damon said that you needed it to take me to school and stuff. We picked it out together. Here, I took a picture of it for you so you didn't have to go out into the cold with your sore leg."

It was indeed a big car. Actually, an SUV of a big car. The dark green Hummer looked huge with Damon standing next to it. There was even a big bow in the roof. She smiled at both her men and kissed them both. Damon's just lasted longer. And might have been even longer, but Connor started to pretend he was throwing up.

They drove her car over to the family home. Everyone was already there since they had spent the night before. Charlie was just getting settled on the big couch when Morgan and the other women came and sat next to her. She knew they were up to something as soon as Taylor sent Byron away. She grinned at Charlie.

"He hates when I'm the dom outside the bedroom. Makes him growl the sexiest sound that does all sorts of delicious things to me. But I digress. We're here about you getting pregnant. Are you yet? Pregnant, I mean?"

Charlie was still trying to get through the whole dom thing when she realized what Taylor had asked her. Did these women ever hear of the word privacy? Her face heated with the knowledge that she could indeed be pregnant right now.

"I don't think so. We...that is to say we kind of...I...why do you want to know?"

"Trying. are you? Good. I hope you're huge when you walk down the aisle. Margaret likes to tell us she hates it, but I think she secretly loves the fact that her sons can't keep it in their pants. Just so you know, I am too. Pregnant. I haven't told anyone but you guys so far. Not even Byr. He's going to have kittens. I wrapped the test up and put it under the tree along with the doctor's report. I'm due in July. If you're trying now, you'll be due in September or October. Cool."

Charlie looked at the other women around her. They were nodding at her as if she'd asked them something. She was sure she hadn't, but they kept nodding all the same. After telling Taylor congratulations, they all started talking about the plans for the upcoming birth of Morgan's and Dane's children and the trial for Gibbons versus Kirkpatrick the Monday after the New Year.

Chapter 22

Damon watched the man sitting at the other table without his attorney. Devin and Charlie sat directly in front of him and the rest of his family was spread out beside him. They had all come to the hearing today to hear why Gibbons had suddenly wanted joint custody of his long lost son. Connor sat to Damon's left. He'd been so nervous this morning that he'd only eaten three helpings of pancakes instead of his usual five. Damon smiled. Feeding this kid was going to be expensive but fun.

Connor didn't look like his father, not really. Connor had grown in the month and a half since he'd been living with him. Most of his pants were already too short and his arms had grown a full five inches, Damon was sure. But he loved it and him.

Connor's hair was lighter than Gibbons' dark brown. That was probably due to the fact that Charlie's was blond. His eyes were an unusual shade of silver-gray that sparked with mischief and humor. There was also a great deal of intelligence there too. When Connor had gone in to be tested for his grade level, he'd tested in the high fourth grade percentile. At nine, Connor would be in the class with a bunch of kids a year or more older than him. Damon carried around the print out of his score in his wallet.

Devin was ready when the proceeds began as soon as Judge James Tyler was seated. He stood just after the room was called to order and began his case. Devin was a sight to see when he was in his professional mood. Damon wondered if anyone would recognize this man over the one who'd had a snowball fight with Connor and the others over the weekend and had been covered in snow while Connor and the others had been clean.

"Mr. Gibbons, it says here you're representing yourself in this matter. Are you sure you want to do that? Counselor Grant is a hell of a lawyer and you know what they say about representing yourself. I can have a court appointed lawyer sit in with you if you want."

Damon was shocked by that. He thought that they had been waiting on his attorney, not that Gibbons was doing it solo. That was just stupid. Damon wouldn't even go to traffic court without either Ronnie or Devin with him.

"Nope. I think I can handle this one. I have the law on my side and we both know that always wins in the end." Damon wasn't sure, but he thought Gibbons winked at Devin.

"Well then let's get this show on the road, shall we? Too nice of a day to be inside, if you ask me. Grant, you can start."

Ronnie leaned over to Damon and whispered in his ear. "Judge Tyler hates pompous asses. And he loves me. Devin is okay in his opinion because he married me, but he isn't going to set well with this guy's attitude. I think this might be fun to watch."

"Your Honor, Mr. Gibbons is claiming that he had no knowledge of the child, Connor Joshua Kirkpatrick, and that his mother, Charlotte Jane Kirkpatrick, kept him from his son. I have documentation that disputes that fact. I have a letter here from Gibbons telling Charlotte that if she tried to tell anyone what had happened on the night of May tenth that no one would believe her. And another letter from him several months later just after he was informed of the pregnancy telling her that he would see her in hell before he got himself attached to a nobody like her. He also suggested that my client have an abortion and rid herself of her bastard."

"That's a lie! I never knew a damned thing. She probably wrote those when she found out I wanted to see my son for the first time," Brody said to the judge.

"Sit down. Gibbons, I don't tolerate stupidity in my court room, nor do I like someone to yell louder than me. Sit your butt down or else. Proceed, Grant, what else you got in your bag of tricks? Hand that stuff over to the bailiff and let me see it as you present."

"Thank you, Your Honor. I have a letter from Hart and Hart, the then attorney firm for the Gibbons family, stating that if my client put Mr. Gibbons' name on the birth certificate, she would be sued. There is also a DNA test that was performed at the insistence of the mother of Brody Phillip Gibbons and the results are a positive match for this man and Connor. You'll see here where Mr. Brody was required to sign for the information."

Everyone watched as the judge read over each sheet as it was handed to him. There wasn't much doubt that Connor was Brody's and that the man had known of his existence. But proving it beyond a shadow of a doubt was what they had to do.

"What do you have to say for yourself, Mr. Gibbons? There's a lot of evidence here that disputes everything you're claiming was done to you. Seems you had every opportunity to claim this boy as yours and you didn't."

"I don't know what to say, Your Honor. It's all lies. I never knew about the boy until I saw his picture in the paper some weeks ago. I also don't believe you should take her word over mine. I'm an upstanding citizen in my town and my family is one of the founders of it. We have money and things like this just don't set right with my family."

Damon wanted to get up and knock the guy on his pompous ass. When Connor reached over and took his hand, he winked at him. Damon couldn't believe how much he loved this kid.

"So you have money and that makes you above the law? I don't think so," Devin said as he referred to his notes again. "I have records here stating that Mr. Gibbons has been sued twice on charges of child support and rape. Each time, Mr. Gibbons has denied being the father even after tests prove the opposite."

"Got anything to say about this, Gibbons? Three kids in four years makes me want to send you to sex ed classes, not that I think you'd pay attention. You should learn to wrap that thing before you go sticking it where you don't intend to pay up." Devin cleared his throat and the judge looked over at Devin then at Connor. "Sorry, kid. Forgot you were here." With a wink, he continued. "You want to explain to me how three times makes you a family man and you don't have any of these kids with you?"

"I don't believe any of them are mine, Your Honor. Women will say anything to get a wealthy man to marry them. And Charlotte was from the wrong part of town anyway. It stands to reason she'd set her sights so high."

"You say that about my momma again and I'll kick your butt. Momma said you weren't nothing but a sperm donna anyway, you mean man. My momma is a good person. Besides, I wouldn't want you as my daddy if you had all the money in the world." The court room burst out into laughter. Even the judge was having a hard time trying to look stern. Damon pulled Connor back to his seat when he had finished yelling at the "sperm donna."

"Your Honor, these charges against my client are ridiculous. Mr. Gibbons was made aware of Connor. His family was aware of him as well. My client has not now, nor has she ever made any kind of financial claim against Mr. Gibbons, and we believe that his current state of affairs is the only reason he is claiming anything now."

"What state of affairs are we talking about, Grant? You think he's in this for a bit of the Grant money? You claiming this boy now because you think something is owed to you?" Judge Tyler turned to Brody so quickly that Damon was startled for a second.

"I want to see my boy, that's all. Those other women had girls. Thomas is my only son and I have missed his early years. I do think that she should have to pay for that, yes. I deserve some sort of compensation for missing his first years. I don't care where she gets the money from. Hell, Your Honor, that lady in the paper is supposed to be a billionaire. She can well afford it."

"Why you dirty, rotten bastard! Your long lost son is Connor, not Thomas you stupid idiot. Let me get this straight, you want my family to pay for your raping me? You think that you should be compensated because I struggled to make ends meet for us so that I could go to college and become someone Connor could be proud of? Because of you, I had to leave home and if you had have just owned up to what you did to me, Anthony wouldn't have kidnapped us."

"This is your fault. I had to drug you to have sex with you in the first place, you stupid cunt. You wouldn't put out another way. And what do you care anyway? You'll have all the money you want, bitch. I just want a little for myself."

The courtroom was silent. Damon looked from Gibbons to the judge. Gibbons didn't seem to see what major mistake he'd made yet. But everyone else in the room did. Devin simply sat down and folded his arms over his chest. Damon was sure if he could see his face, that Devin would have his brow raised to his hairline. This was going to be good.

"You drugged Ms. Kirkpatrick to have sex with her. You know that's rape, don't you?" Gibbons paled as the judge continued. "This birth certificate says that she was only seventeen when she had Connor. And according to the records here, you were twenty-two. That's going to cost you, boy. I don't take kindly to—"

"I didn't rape the bitch. She wouldn't put out and I wanted her. Simple as that. I have money and money talks."

"You'll not interrupt me again, you sorry excuse for a turd! This is my playground and my rules. Sit down and shut up. Grant! How much money does this idiot have? I want to know right down to the last penny."

"With his holding in his family's business, property owned by him personally, the trust fund that he only gets interest from until he turns thirty-five, and his job with the company, Mr. Gibbons' net worth is just under three million dollars. He does have three outstanding debts that total more than that, however. It seems Mr. Gibbons has a bit of a gambling problem."

"Good. Bailiff, take this man into custody. Grant, I want you to file a claim against his worth and seize his money and funds. I don't take kindly to stupid people and less to ones who rape children."

"Wait! Why am I being arrested? I didn't do anything wrong. She kept me from my son Corby. I want my money!"

Gibbons fought against the bailiff, trying to cuff him as he tried to reason with the judge. Connor slipped past Damon and stood next to the man that had helped create him.

"My name is Connor Joshua Kirkpatrick, you stupid man. And I think you're a weenie. I hope you go to jail forever."

Brody lunged at Connor, but before Brody could touch Connor, Damon hit the man in the nose. Blood poured over his shirt and jacket as he fell to the floor.

"You touch my son again and I'll make you regret it for the rest of your life. And I don't care how much money you think you might have." Damon pulled away from his brothers as they held him back. After straightening his tie, Damon reached out and took Connor's hand as they went to Charlie.

~~~

Connor kept looking at Damon on the way home. He wasn't sure what to make of Mr. G, but he was happy that the whole thing was over. He didn't like that his momma had cried, but Jamie had told him she was happy. Connor didn't think he'd ever understand girls. Wasn't even sure he wanted to try. They were just weird.

But Damon had called him his son. Not just between them like he was calling him son like it was his name or something, but said that he was his son. He'd even had to be held back like he was going to hurt Mr. G. Connor looked up in the mirror again and noticed that Damon was looking back at him too.

"Connor, you don't have to worry about that man trying to get you or anything. Devin said he'll be put away for a long time. Gibbons won't be bothering you or your mother ever again."

"Yes, sir, I know that. Uncle Devin told me. He said that Mr. G was going to pay for his mistakes like he should have a long time ago. And I asked Momma. She said I wasn't a mistake like I thought he meant. She said I was a blessing." Connor wasn't sure what that meant either, but if his momma told him that with one of her happy smiles then he believed her. Sometimes when he talked with the grownups in his life now, he thought it was easier to ask his momma what they meant.

They pulled up in front of the restaurant that they were going to celebrate in and Connor didn't jump out like he normally did. He had a lot on his mind and he figured that he'd feel better if he just asked Damon rather than let it stew around in his head. When his momma turned to look at him, he grinned at her. It was a fake grin, but she didn't seem to notice.

"Momma, do you think I can talk to Damon for a minute? Alone. I have...I want to ask him something about ...about my new computer. Guy stuff, you know?"

Connor felt bad for lying to his mom, but he didn't want to talk to Damon with her around. She'd never make him feel bad, but he would all the same. She just nodded her head, kissed Damon, and got out of the new car. She went over to Byron and Taylor and they went inside the restaurant.

"You want to come up here and talk to me or do you want to do it from back there? I can see you better if you come up here. Either way is fine with me."

"You called me your son. Today in the law place you called me your son to that man. I'm not, you know."

Connor squirmed in his seat when Damon didn't say anything for a few minutes. When Damon turned around and looked at Connor, he wanted to squirm more but sat on his fingers instead. Connor finally looked up at him.

"Did that bother you? Or was there something else? I thought we were a family, but if you don't want me to call you that...well, I was going to say that would be fine, but I like thinking you're my son."

"Meggie calls Aunt Cait Mom and I know she's not really her kid. Jacob and Little Jim call Grandma Mom, but I know they aren't her kids either. I want you to be my dad. I never had one before. But if you didn't really want that but said that to Mr. G to make him think you were, then I want you to tell me."

"Connor, before I answer you, why do you call Devin and the others Uncle? Why do you call my mom Grandma? They aren't really that to you, not yet at any rate. Why haven't you called me Uncle Damon?"

Connor had thought about that. He had never actually given any thought to calling the others Uncle or Aunt. It just sort of fell out of his mouth one day and when nobody told him to not do it anymore, he kept doing it. But Damon? Damon hadn't felt like an uncle.

"I don't know. You never seemed like an uncle to me. You were always bossy like my momma, I guess. And Meggie calls the others Uncle and Aunt and well, no body said I couldn't call them that so I kept it up. Should I stop doing it, you think?"

"No, I don't. I think it would hurt them if you did. They love you as much as if you'd been born into our family anyway. I have something for you. Your mom and I were going to give it to you later, but now is better."

Connor reached for the large blue folder. He opened it up and read the first few lines of the neatly typed pages. He didn't understand all the words, but he did get the meaning.

"It says here you want to adopt me. That you want me to become a Grant like you and Momma when she marries you. Momma knows that you want to do this? She okay with it?"

"Yes. I would never have been able to file the petition without her permission. I decided that I love you too much for you not to be my son both in name and in my heart. You don't have to change your name if you want to go through this. That would be entirely up to you."

Connor didn't answer. He didn't care if his name was Pink Petunia as long as Damon loved him too. Connor looked out the window. He just had one more thing to ask.

"What if you and Momma have kids together? You gonna wish you didn't have me around then I bet. I'm not really your son and that one would be."

"Yes, you are my son, Connor. Whether you sign those papers or not, you'll always be my son. Your mom and I are planning to have other children. Yes, it's true that they'll be of my blood where you won't. Other people have children of their blood that they don't love half as much as I do you. But Connor, I choose you to be my son. I want you to be my first born with all my heart."

Connor looked back at the man who meant everything in the world to him and decided he couldn't love him anymore if he were is real dad. Taking a deep breath, he stuck out his small hand and asked his final thing.

"Can I call you Dad?"

Chapter 23

One year later

"Connor, will you hurry up? Christ, your parents are going to kill us. We were supposed to leave ten minutes ago. Where's your coat?"

Connor looked at the frazzled woman standing at the bottom of the stairs. His aunt Dane looked like she could be in one of her pretty people magazines. She was holding one of his cousins, Alan, and the other one, Anna, was still lying on the couch half in and half out of her coat that looked like a bag. The twins had been a surprise to everyone, including Uncle Jamie and Aunt Dane.

"Momma said that she would wait for us. I don't think she was supposed to have the baby until later. Dad said she would be in labor for another five hours. Is that all it takes? You just tell the baby to wait and it does?"

"Not in my experience, no. Can you see if you can figure out that stupid car seat for me? I swear that Pi changes them out just to frustrate me."

"Missy Dane, I do not. You just don't work it right. I tell you five hundred time to put kid in seat in house then take to car. Much easier when you can get to front of it. Let me show you again."

Connor tried not to let Dane see him laugh, but it was funny that a woman as smart as his aunt Dane was couldn't figure out a car seat buckle. When she winked at him over Pi's head, he nearly fell over. She knew how to do it. Aunt Dane was just playing with Pi. He laughed this time. These two were the best part of this family some days.

"Pi, are you coming with us to the hospital, or are you staying here and cooking? I think James said that he would have them all come here if you wanted to cook for everyone. It's up to you, but you have to hurry. I'm running late. Again."

"You run nowhere fast, Missy Dane. You take time off or I tell Mister Jamie to beat you with cane. Someday I want to take cane to you. You work too hard. I stay and cook, but I no like you running you self in to mud. Bad for your hair."

It took Connor a full minute to translate that one. When he started to tell his grandma Pi that she meant "running into the ground," he thought about her asking about why anyone would want to run into the ground and decided her way was just fine. That was another thing he loved about coming here. He got to learn a whole new language, Pi-isms.

After they were all loaded in the van, Connor thought about the past year. His momma and Damon had gone on their honeymoon in Paris after they got married on Valentine's Day. When they came back, his momma went to work for Damon because Ms. Tansy, the nurse who worked for Damon forever, had died in her sleep one night. That was the first funeral Connor had ever been to.

Then two weeks later, Aunt Morgan had her baby. A cute little girl named Cybil. She looked just like her momma and Cybil's brothers wouldn't let anyone touch her except Connor. They thought he was cool. Then Aunt Dane had the twins. Uncle Jamie still talked about the argument he'd had with Damon in the delivery room over that one. Uncle Jamie thought that Damon should have told them there were twins and Dad pointed out that when you say you want the entire birth experience to be a surprise, then that's what you got. A surprise. Connor didn't know why he thought so, but he could almost swear that Dad hadn't told them on purpose.

Then he'd had to go to his next funeral two months later. Grandda had died. He'd been out in the yard mowing the grass and had had a heart attack. Dad said that he'd not suffered but had gone quickly.

Connor didn't think his grandma was ever going to be the same after that. She still worked and all, but he could tell that she was really sad. Connor had been going over to her house more and more lately. He liked her very much and she had the coolest stories about her family. Connor hoped she wouldn't die too. He liked having a grandma. Jacob and Little Jim had taken it hard too. He liked his cousins and they all played together. But like Grandma, they didn't seem the same anymore.

Connor's momma worked for Aunt Dane and for his dad. His momma was so happy all the time now he couldn't help be happy with her. When the first child support check had come in the mail a week or so after Grandda had died, she'd sat him down and told him what she wanted him to do with his money.

"It's all yours, Connor. And it's no small amount either. I'd like for you to save at least half of it for your education. It's going to be expensive and you might need the extra money when you go there. I know you're really smart and you'll probably get a scholarship, but that doesn't mean that you won't have expenses. All right?"

Dad had told him that he'd paid for his own education. That even though is parents could well afford it, they'd made sure their sons knew the value of working for something. Momma thought that was a good rule to follow too.

Connor took the check from his momma. Uncle Devin told him that Brody had to pay back child support for Connor until he was caught up, and a monthly amount. Mr. G was in jail now. Not only had he gotten in trouble with raping his momma, but there had been other women who had come forward and said he'd done the same to them. He was in a lot of trouble, Uncle Devin explained.

The check was for a little over five thousand dollars. If Connor saved half, he'd still have a lot of money to spend if he wanted to. But Connor had a debt to be paid. And he was ready to start paying it forward.

"Grandma said she'd help me set up a fund. I want to take the other half of this money and help little kids like me to get away from mean men like Mr. O. Aunt Ronnie said she'd help me get more money with donation so that I can give it to moms and kids that need to run away like you and I did. She said that it's easy when it's a good cause."

"That's a wonderful idea, Connor. I'm very proud of you. You'll need a good name for your foundation.

Something that says it all, something people can remember."

He had been working on that since she'd told him and, now all this time later, he still didn't have a good name. He had to hurry now. His grandma had told him that she would announce his foundation and what it was doing at the next charity event in five days.

They arrived at the hospital to find Uncle Jamie waiting for them. He hurried to the car and took one of the twins out and threw her expertly over his shoulder as he unbuckled her brother. Pi would have been so proud of him. When they got to the labor floor, the twins were taken from him and settled over the laps of the people sitting there waiting for his brother or sister to be born.

Connor sat next to his grandma while she held Alan on her lap and fed him a bottle. She looked to be really enjoying the baby so he didn't beg to hold him as he normally would have. Connor did touch his little fingers.

"Got a name yet? I've been thinking of possibilities and there are any number of them you can use. 'Kids' Way' is nice. Then there's another favor of mine called 'Kid Forward.'"

Connor suddenly had it. He thought it was perfect. And he hoped his grandma thought so too.

"I got it, Grandma. If you like it, that is. The 'Daniel Parker Foundation.' I think Grandda would have liked it too, don't you?"

Grandma didn't answer because just then Dad came out of the back room and looked right at him. Connor stood up and walked to him as his dad dropped to his knees. Connor was worried at first. Dad was crying and that made him scared.

"Connor, you have a little sister. She is beautiful. As beautiful as your mom. Your mom wants you to come back and see her before the others do. Are you ready to be a big brother?"

"Yes, sir. I'm so ready. I get to pick her name. You guys said if it was a girl, I could pick her name. I got it, Dad. Her name is Mackenzie Jorden Grant. I'm going to call her Mac for short. What do you think?"

"Connor, I think it's perfect. Let's go so you can tell her. Connor, I love you very much."

"I love you too, Dad. I love you very much."

About The Author

I woke up one morning and decided to give play time to the people in my head who were keeping me awake. Little did I know that they would be so relentless and want their time right now! I wrote for the pure joy of it and to entertain my family and friends. But mostly it was to get more than an hour of sleep without a story playing out. Of course, the more I write, the more they want. So…well, as a result of sleepless days (I work through the night as a gun toting grandma – nope not a vigilantly but an armed security guard) I have lots of stories written.

Hello! My name is Kathi Barton and I'm an author. I have been married to my very best friend Sonny for at times seems several lifetimes – in a good way, honey. And together we have three wonderful children and then the ones we brought into the world - Paul and Dale Barton, Jason and Wendy Barton and Danielle and Ben Conklin. They have given us seven of the greatest treasures on Earth. They don't live at home seven days a week! No, seriously, seven grandchildren – Gavin, Spring, Ben, Trinity, Sarah, Kelly and Kian.

www.ingramcontent.com/pod-product-compliance
Lightning Source LLC
Chambersburg PA
CBHW020610180626
46810CB00007B/2717